Live
the Gift

Stories

Scott Thomas

Contents

Introduction

The life of faith is the life of story.

Sometimes that's obvious. Anyone who has spent time reading the Bible, for instance, can't help but notice that it's less a philosophical treatise than a collection of tales about God's imperfect people doing the best they can to imagine the unimaginable. We try to wrap our minds around a power and a presence irretrievably far beyond us, and the way our great gray brains work, that translates into telling ourselves stories about talking bushes and amazing dinners of bread and fish. (Which is not to say that the biblical stories aren't *true*, a word that gives fits to theologians and those seeking black-letter law, rather than grace, from their God.) This impulse toward the holy story helps to explain why we find the gospel accounts of Jesus' life so engaging. To have a flesh-and-blood God to watch and learn from – how can we *not* love the words of Matthew, Mark, Luke and John?

Sometimes the faith story isn't so obvious. In our own lives, it's tempting to take the everydayness as it comes. Often it's only in moments of crisis – the end of a marriage or a life, great pain or great uncertainty – that we recognize our own years as forming a story. Look at your life – it's an unfolding story! You know the beginning; you know the story up till now. You know the plot with its unexpected turns, its surprising revelations, its tepid stretches of description, its occasional vivid action. Only the ending remains to be told, a telling that starts today.

I come to the stories in this volume with a simple premise: The biblical stories, and the stories we live out and tell about our contemporaries, are really parts of God's overarching story. Like a masterful musical composition whose signature theme and variations crop up again and again, God's story finds expression in the infinite variety of human life in all times. Only the ending remains to be told.

Part 1 consists of stories set in the present; each is keyed to a scripture passage that may deepen the experience of reading. Part 2 is a series of biblical stories told from a human perspective, trying to go deeper into the experience of the biblical characters than the sometimes dispassionate language of the scriptures allows.

Part 3 is a single piece of historical fiction, imagining life in the Oneida Community of upstate New York in the 1860s. The Oneida Community, led by the charismatic John Humphrey Noyes, was one of several faith-based experiments in communal living of the mid-19th century. What fascinates historians is Noyes' free-love sexual philosophy and its intersection with the agape love of a faith community.

Except for "Home Talk," these stories were written for the faith community I am privileged to serve as pastor, Amherst Community Church in Snyder, N.Y. I am grateful for the support and patience of this wonderful congregation's good people, and it is to them that this work is dedicated.

Rev. Scott Thomas
Buffalo
January 2010

Inviting
the Story In

What Child Is This?

L u k e   1

Outside the sun was without mercy, but under the simple roof the cool was a blessing. Hot for this time of year, she thought, waiting for his return from the carpentry shop where they paid just less than a living wage. She was working on dinner: bread and olive oil, and tonight a precious few scraps of meat.

It was a special night. He would protest about the meat – they couldn't afford luxuries, he had told her more than once – but when he heard the news, he would not think about the dinner. He would think about the future. She was sure of it.

Their engagement was according to law and custom – mostly, anyway. He was a good man and had studied enough law to know what was right. But this, this news, it was beyond custom and outside the law. She played the conversation in her mind like a candy between lips and tongue, playing with it, wishing it to come out right. If only she could be sure he wouldn't be ashamed. Or angry.

She put down the strand of bread dough. Her hand went to her abdomen. Only the faintest swelling betrayed her secret, what she now had to tell this man who was to be her husband.

Not long now until his homecoming. If only he could see the joy she felt growing inside her. But she was faint with fear.

♦ ♦ ♦

Fear was something they lived with, ever since the soldiers had come. Not that the occupying forces had bothered them, though there were rumors of women attacked and houses burned for sport. They even said they were there to preserve the peace. But it was peace on their terms. No one dared talk back. A faraway ruler had sent them, and his military was too strong to resist.

No, the soldiers didn't hurt them. But their very presence, the weapons on their shoulder, their eyes that followed every movement, those were oppression enough. On the way to market they watched; on the way home they watched; they watched as doors opened and windows swung wide in the morning, they watched as the last flame was extinguished at night.

Other rumors spoke of an end to all this, the hope that God would send a leader to fight their way out of desperation. But if this was God's will, why hadn't it happened already? They were left to live as best they could, work and marry and cobble together families. Everywhere, the watchful eyes of the soldiers. No one knew what would come next. But something had to give.

◆ ◆ ◆

He was home. She heard his feet on the stones, then he was there. He held her a moment. The smell of dinner turned his head.

"Meat?" he said. "Have I not told you –"

"You need to sit down," she said. "There is news." He could tell by the tone of her voice that he had better do what he was told. She sat beside him, close the way he liked it, and took his hand, and watched his eyes, and gave him the news.

When she told the story later, she was inclined to soften the words that he said next. Times were hard, she would say. I understand his pain.

But without the worn edges of nostalgia, his words were like flint.

"A child," he said. "A child for us. When we are just beginning our life together. This was not my intention."

"Nor mine," she said softly. "But God makes choices. God has chosen this."

"And has God chosen misery for us, then?" he said. "Even this little dinner we cannot afford. A child! How are we to feed three on wages that barely keep two above ground?"

"It is chosen," she said, a little stubbornly. "It cannot be undone."

He paced awhile, silent. She dared not speak.

"Something else," he said. "You see the soldiers there. Is this a world to bring a child into? I see nothing better on this road. I see no hope. For us this is so, and we cannot change it. But for an infant to grow into this pain! Better that he were never born. Better that he were never conceived."

"It is chosen," she said again. "*We* are chosen."

They ate the food in silence. When he left the next morning, he took a change of clothes. He did not look back.

◆ ◆ ◆

On the night of the third day he was gone, a dream came to her.

It began with a frightful vision: a landscape like her own little town's, but where huts and markets had stood, there were only bones, piled like lumber, a macabre community of loss. In the dream she walked the streets of this town of bones. They were full of people she knew, and they all went about their business the same as always. No one seemed to be bothered that their world was built on grief.

In the dream she felt the child within her, felt him kick (or was that her waking belly and her living child?). And that kick quickened in her a resolve. She would leave the town of bones. She would find a better place for this child.

But there was no escape. Soldiers blocked the one road out; she considered setting out across the desert, but when she tried it, dunes of sand rose impossibly high before her. She climbed, but the sand slipped beneath her feet and choked her lungs, and finally she knew there was no escape.

The child inside her moved again, and she turned. And then, in the strange logic of dreams, she saw the same town, her town, with new eyes. Eyes of a different vision. Where there had been only death, only the bones of the past and the rigor of the present, now she squinted against a brilliant white light. The huts, the markets, even her kinsfolk making their usual rounds – all of them as if they were made of this brightness, a light like the relentless sun, but now solid and real, the houses framed and roofed in light, the people incandescent in their ordinariness.

And in the dream, she looked down and saw that she herself was made of this brilliant light, and she felt its cool white presence in her heart and her head and her belly. And again the infant moved within her.

◆ ◆ ◆

The next day he returned. She saw him a ways off. He was carrying something, big and heavy, covered in military camouflage cloth he had scavenged. She waited inside, unsure what would come through the door.

He was sweating as he placed his bundle carefully on the worn floor. "For you," he said. His body showed the tension of their last encounter, but his eyes were bright. Hopeful. His was a gift of peace.

She looked up at him, questioning. He motioned toward the package. She put her hand on the cloth and then slowly drew it aside.

A wooden cradle, beautiful in its symmetry and so carefully polished that even in the dim light of indoors, it glowed. At its head was carved the figure of the sun, its beams reaching straight and true, power and light that would watch over the child who would be rocked to sleep in this cradle. *Their* child.

"I have spoken wrongly," he said. "It is hard times. Supporting a child – I don't know how I can. *If* I can."

"But he is not a sorrow, this child. He is a gift. He will be the finest child of al-Anbar province."

They sat close together, looking at the cradle.

"You said that we are chosen. God is with us, then. We will bring a child into this world where soldiers patrol. In this life I have not found hope. But you have found it for me. In this child is hope where there was none. In this child, we remake the world."

◆ ◆ ◆

When she told the story later, she made little mention of labor and delivery, the exhaustion, the pain. When she told the story, she skipped right to the ending: the infant in his mother's arms, and then in his father's cradle. The child of promise, a promise that lives in every child, but somehow in this red-faced infant, a promise that drew all the creative power of hope to himself, and let it shine like the rays of the life-giving sun, before the powerful, before the poor.

Live the Gift

2 Corinthians 4:4-7

It was on the day of the big ice storm that the old woman gave me a gift of words. I was finishing a twelve-hour shift at Holy Name Hospital, where I am a nurse. A male nurse, if that's important to you. It is to a lot of people. They look at me sometimes like a freak, like I should be wearing a dress or something. Maybe they watch too many *Marcus Welby* reruns. But I have nothing to apologize for. The money's good, and hey, the fringe benefits – I meet lots of women.

Besides, if you want to know the truth, I kind of like being the odd man out. It's a weird world, you know what I mean? Why force yourself to fit in? Better to make your own way, and anybody doesn't like it, tough. You've only got one life, might as well live it your way.

The only thing is, it hasn't been going so well lately. Winter does that to me. Might be that seasonal depression that comes from living under clouds for twenty-eight days out of every month. They say you can sit under a big light panel and glow your way out of it, but that seems like a lot of trouble to me. That's the thing about depression – it kind of paralyzes you. Some days it feels like you can't even get out of bed to take your meds, much less set up a tanning booth in your living room.

And Holy Name Hospital doesn't help much, either. Oh, it's a place to work, and I guess good things happen there. Maybe we don't make a lot of miracles happen, but people get cured every so often, and mostly we don't make them any worse off. But I've been doing this now for seven years – turning patients, moving patients, taking patients to X-ray, listening to patients gripe about the food and the beds and their doctors. There's a chart on the wall for pain management, so patients can say how much it hurts, and there are faces on it – a smiley face down around 1 and 2, a face with kind of a grimace in the middle of the scale, and up at 10 a face with what looks like a splitting headache. I see that chart in every room, and I can't stop thinking that my face is never up there. My face would be a perfect circle with no eyes or nose or mouth. That's where I am as I put in my hours at Holy Name Hospital. Blank. Nothing.

But that has changed. I want to tell you my story.

It happened on the day of the big ice storm. Like I said, I was near the end of my shift on Ten West, where the post-surgical patients go. I was making a last round when I saw all the staff gathered at the big window in the waiting lounge.

You could hear the rattling against the window. Sleet or freezing rain – I could never understand the difference. Whatever it was, it was making for plenty of trouble. Even up where we were, you could see what a mess the traffic was. I saw a car smashed into a Metro bus. There was another one plowed into a light pole, knocking it over and sending steam pouring from under the hood. As I watched, an SUV slid sideways across three lanes, and it looked like bumper pool down there.

Great, I thought. It'll take me an hour to get home, assuming I can get there in one piece. Assuming I don't slide right back into Holy Name Hospital with a concussion or something.

I went back to the job, working my way down the far hall first. Vital signs, checking the incisions, watching for signs of infection or worse. If you're in the hospital these days, generally you're really sick. The easy ones are all outpatient now. It makes it harder on everybody.

I was making good time until I got to 1018. Mrs. LaRue, age 88, hip replacement, two days post-op. She'd be out of there soon, off to a rehab place where they'd yell at her like a football coach until she got the hang of her new bionic body. She liked to talk, I remembered that. Today was no different.

"You're late," she said, but there was no malice in it. "It's usually 3:30 that you're here."

"I was watching the ice storm," I said, motioning out the window. But she was in Bed A, by the door; neither of us could see down to the street.

"Oh, what fun," she said. "Ice is always so beautiful. I always loved it when an ice storm came. When I was a girl ..."

"That's because you don't have to drive in it," I put in. "Not all that much fun then. I'll be lucky to be home in time for *Jeopardy*."

She considered that. She had never turned on her hospital TV. Didn't read much, either. Just lay there with her thoughts and her memories.

"I'm going home tomorrow," Mrs. LaRue said. "My daughter is coming to get me."

Might be, might not. How many times I've heard something like that, and the daughter turns out to be in California with no intention of bothering about her mom. Leaving everything to the hired help.

"That's good, Mrs. LaRue," I said. "Now blow into this tube and show me how strong your lungs are."

She did, and handed it back to me with a look of pride. She wasn't going down without a fight.

"My daughter's coming for me," she repeated, "and I won't see you tomorrow. Won't see you anymore at all."

"Well, you just get yourself back on your feet," I started to say, but before I got halfway through it, she stopped me.

"I want to give you something." She opened the drawer in the little bedside table, rummaged around a little and pulled something out. "Here. I want you to have this."

It was a tiny wooden box, no bigger than a plum and ornately carved. The carvings had worn away some over the years, like somebody had held onto it tight.

"Well, thank you, Mrs. LaRue, but we're not really allowed to accept gifts from patients," I said. The box felt heavy in my hand. Solid.

"Then it will have to be our little secret, won't it?" she said. She closed my fingers around the wood. "You need this more than I do. You have a lot of time to get it right."

I didn't understand, but I didn't push it. The clock was running out on my day.

"Our little secret," I said. "Thank you. Get well, now." As I left the room, she was smiling at some hidden thought.

◆ ◆ ◆

Before I went home I had my usual coffee-and-a-cigarette in the cafeteria. Say what you want about the food, the coffee is good. I read the paper and toyed with the little wooden box, turning it over, trying to fathom what had possessed this woman to bequeath it to me. Was it some antique she thought I could sell on eBay? An engagement ring box? As if I had somebody lined up. I wish. Was there some treasure inside?

Anticipation feels alive, so it was a long time before I opened the box. When I did, I was disappointed. No treasure. No diamonds, no gold. Just a tiny scrap of paper, yellowed with age, and seven words printed in a simple, exacting hand:

Good news.

Great joy.

Live the gift.

I thought about that but couldn't make much sense of it. Good news – OK, what was it? Certainly nothing in the newspaper qualified. Great joy – well, I didn't know as I'd recognize that if I saw it. It had been a long time since I felt joyful about anything.

And "Live the gift." This gift? This little box? These words?

Good news.

Great joy.

Live the gift.

I thought about going back and asking Mrs. LaRue to explain, but I didn't. When she gave me the box, there was an air of finality to it. A one-way gift. Apparently she figured I would know what to do with it.

Well, there she was wrong. I stuck the box in my coat pocket and headed out into the winter air.

◆ ◆ ◆

The garage attendant almost laughed at me. "Don't even try it, buddy," he said. "It's total gridlock out there. They can't even get the salt trucks through. You get in that car now, you'll be sitting there for hours."

Great. Now what?

I decided to walk it. Maybe a half-hour, but it made more sense than risking the drive. I started up Center Street.

The garage man was right – traffic was a disaster. Between the wrecks and the spinouts, nobody could go anywhere. People were abandoning their cars and heading for the sidewalks, briefcases and babies in hand.

The ice had stopped falling. Even the clouds had cleared away, and suddenly it struck me that the sun was out. It felt warm on my face. People were helping each other over the snowbanks. Kids were sliding around and laughing, and their parents were trying to stay upright and laughing at themselves when they went sprawling across the slick ice. It was a pain, but it was an adventure.

Somehow lines came to me from a poem my tenth-grade English teacher had made us memorize. The poem was called "A Christmas Storm," and from nowhere in particular the words floated into consciousness:

Drainpipes and eaves and scintillant fans
Of bush and tree turned emblems of themselves;
Where every twig is one and three, itself,
Its chrysalis in ice transparent ...

"The rarely tinseled treasures of the world," the poet had said – everything its own self, but coated now in ice and somehow that made it special. Made it Christmas, like tinsel.

I looked and sure enough I saw tinsel all around me: in the telephone wires, in the battered cars frozen in place, in the way the bricks of the buildings smoothed into a glistening run of ice. But above all I saw the trees, the trees whose bare branches had always been for me evidence of winter's sad lifelessness. I saw the trees painted in translucence, the ice precisely brushed on every twig by some mad artist. They rain-bowed the pale winter sun, like the biggest chandelier you ever saw, and for a moment I could not walk, I could not speak, I could scarcely breathe.

Good news.

Great joy.

Live the gift.

Then I walked, and marveled at the miracle of walking, and thought of Mrs. LaRue and her new hip and the words she had left behind. For me. For all who can find room in their lives for a gift of mystery and miracle.

It's all around us. I realize that now.

This is my story. Believe it or don't. But whatever you do, hear that good news. Feel that great joy. And live the gift, a gift that comes when you least expect it, a gift that opens like a little box to reveal the treasures of this world, dressed in their every-day tinsel, more beautiful than they have any right to be.

Reversal
of Fortune

Luke 16:19-31

1 Timothy 6:6-11

The sound of steel doors closing. That's the worst, Sherry thinks as she lies on her thin mattress that first night. It's a sharp sound, a harsh sound, and there is a finality to it that is unsettling. She is used to the big wooden front door at her house, and the comforting solid thud it makes as it closes. And the screen doors at the cottage, a sound that to her always meant summer, even now that the family is long gone.

But in prison there isn't much wood, and certainly no screens. Steel, mostly, and concrete, and linoleum for an accent. Sherry sighs, and tries to settle into some sort of comfort on the metal-frame bed. Eighteen months behind these walls. She has always been tough – couldn't have made it in the business she did, in discount tires, without staying tough. But this is like nothing she had ever faced. She can hear something skittering by, down on the floor. Eighteen months. God help her.

And for what? The injustice of it is the worst. A number on line 37 that probably should have been on line 42. Not a mistake, exactly; she knew what she was doing; she always did. It was more like creative accounting. Ledger-demain. Sherry smiles. Well, she deserved the best, didn't she? The stockholders could take two cents less in dividend for once. The workers could get by on last year's wages. She had needs. Servants to pay, the wardrobe to keep up, on and on.

Then the trial, all that hoopla, and now this: The discount tire queen of New England, living like a common criminal in a space eight feet by six.

She lies there, her mind racing, as the hours drag by. By 4 o'clock, she is in a fitful sleep.

• • •

"Head count!"

The voice jolts her awake. She had been warned it would be like this: 6 o'clock every morning you had to stand and deliver, show that you hadn't slipped out between the bars overnight. Ridiculous.

The guard stops in front of her cell. So young! Here she is, fifty-something, and he's on the childhood side of twenty. A wave of sadness breaks inside her. She isn't sure why.

"Randolph?"

"That's me."

He looks at her, and a shock of recognition plays on his face. She has seen it before: in restaurants, on the street. Her face was on TV a lot, in the trial but, before that, in her commercials. It was men who bought tires, and she knew a woman's face sold things. She didn't mind using her charm.

"It's an honor, ma'am."

Sherry says nothing.

The boy hesitates, then walks on down the cellblock. Sherry can hear the names being called and imagines the boy's pencil checking them off methodically on his clipboard. His handwriting is spiky, agitated. So young. She has a son not much older than he. Or had. As her company grew and demanded even nights and weekends, Sean had drifted away. He had declined to testify as a character witness at the trial, and she hasn't heard from him since.

It is two hours till breakfast, another of the small indignities she is discovering about prison life. She wonders how good the coffee is. Do they even serve coffee in prison?

How is she going to endure this for a year and a half?

◆ ◆ ◆

The boy is a regular on D block, it turns out. Some days later, in the recreation room, Sherry finds him at the door, shifting his weight and watching the clock.

"I don't even know your name," she says to him.

"Not important, ma'am," the boy says.

"I like to know whom I'm taking orders from."

The boy scratches his ear. It's like Captain Kangaroo has left the TV and is standing in front of him. He doesn't know what to make of it. Finally he relents.

"It's Fletcher."

"Your *real* name."

He hesitates. "Walter."

"Where you from, Walter?"

"I live over in Lake Carmel. It's a little ways to this place, but the money's good, and it's only for a little while. I'm going to school come September."

"What for?"

"Criminal justice. It's this, only with a degree. It was my father's idea. He's got more money than God, but he has this idea that people should work for a living, no matter if they have to or not. I guess I won't be seeing much of his money anytime soon."

"Kind of a contradiction in terms, isn't it?"

"Ma'am?"

"Criminal justice. Kind of like jumbo shrimp, you know?"

Walter smiles in spite of himself. They had told him not to let the prisoners get to him, warned him not to get too close. But this notorious woman, well, he likes her. Even though she has money and he doesn't. Even though she's in his father's league. The league of criminal gentlemen, he thinks bitterly.

· · ·

"Walter!" Sherry summons the boy in the exercise yard, where a few sullen women are throwing a ball and the others gather in small groups, looking furtive.

"Ma'am?"

"I can't stand these pajamas they make you wear. If I give you some money, could you get me something decent to wear?"

"That's standard issue, ma'am. I can't do that."

"Look," Sherry says. "There's a fabric store in that mall down the road. I've lived my whole life in linen suits. At least get me a swatch of good Irish linen. I just want to feel it between my fingers. Or maybe some purple brocade. I always loved purple. It's so drab here."

"I can't. I'm sorry."

Sherry takes a few steps in the fading light. She can see the guard towers, see the binoculars watching. There are rifles.

"Walter, this is killing me. I'm serious. I cannot survive this. You don't know how hard it is. I need you to help me."

She sees that the boy looks embarrassed.

"Ma'am, I could lose my job. I need the money for college."

"Oh, right. Your father the cheapskate."

"Besides," Walter says, "I think you're wrong. I know how hard it is."

"But you can go home every day! You can get out of here. You have your freedom."

The boy manages a wry smile. "I go home and you know what I do? I have to check in through the guard to even get onto my street. A gated community, they call it, but there's another contradiction in terms for you, ma'am, because there ain't no community. Not really. Plenty of gates to keep the riffraff out, at least that's the concept, but there's no *there* there. People stay inside, and they lock their doors. Anybody comes to that gate without ID, they want to sic the dogs on 'em."

Silence.

Sherry thinks of her estate outside Boston; the compound, that's what the press had called it. If she ever gets out of this prison, she will serve her house arrest there. She thinks of the walls and the gates and the motion sensors and the security lights. She remembers the quiet after Don left her.

"I can't wait to get out of there," the boy continues. "At least in school there will be people who will talk to each other. My cousin is at Duke, and he talks about sitting around with a case of Bud and a huge bowl of popcorn, and they talk all night long. Sometimes that's what you need."

"Popcorn?"

"I mean it. People are starving for each other. *I'm* starving."

A buzzer sounds, and she joins the line to go back inside. She doesn't talk to anyone. She is thinking about her living room, where the vacuum marks stay on the carpet for days and the leather sofa is uncreased by human behinds. She will be back there soon enough.

• • •

And it is there, fourteen months later (good behavior), where she hears the mail truck and walks out to the road. She is allowed that much, under house arrest: a daily walk to check the mail.

There is a package the size of a basketball, wrapped in grocery-bag paper, from some obscure town in Pennsylvania and forwarded to her by her office. The mail truck is gone.

Sherry sits down outside the gate and tears open the wrapping. There is a note, unsigned, but in familiar spiky handwriting.

"Remember," it says.

And sealed in a plastic bag, a double handful of white popcorn.

The air is clear; autumn has painted the trees red and yellow, a day for holding hands and walking together and smelling the earth.

Sherry looks up the road and down the road. There is no one.

She goes through the gate, locking it carefully behind her, and heads for the house.

Plenty

John 10:10

It had been a long workweek, and Brenda walked home with her usual Friday-night feeling of exhaustion and dread. Exhaustion, because her work as a para-legal at Dewey & Howe seemed to drain more life out of her every day. Paralegal – a fancy word that meant she helped people sue each other more efficiently. Car crashes, slip-and-falls, construction accidents, divorced parents suing over how often they got to see their kids – she did it all. She was good at it, too, able to help people see their way through the legal

mumbo-jumbo and get what they wanted from a judge. But she couldn't shake the feeling that her work didn't matter one bit in the grand scheme of things. So Insurance Company A paid the big bucks, and Insurance Company B helped its bottom line. What was that to her?

And then dread. It was Friday night, and in the middle of a great city full of interesting people, Brenda was alone. She had no plans for Friday night. She had no plans for Saturday. Sunday she planned to spend grocery shopping and steeling herself for another week at Dewey & Howe. She couldn't bring herself to imagine another kind of weekend. She walked the dozen blocks to her apartment past the neon joys of the city, and it was all painted in gray, gray, gray.

She was putting her keycard in the lock of her building when she heard it: a whimper. She looked down, and at first she saw nothing. Then – over beneath the bush – a kind of a balled-up shape. She bent closer, and the shape lifted its head. It was a middle-size dog, of no particular breed or maybe a few breeds, scruffy, dirty, and so malnourished that its ribs showed.

Brenda looked around. No owner in sight. She looked at the dog again. No collar. She touched the dog on its shoulder, and it looked her right in the eye. Brenda could almost see the question there. She was a woman of good order, a woman who planned carefully and avoided impulses. But at that moment, it was almost like somebody else was making the decision. She scooped up the dog, hurried past the big sign in the lobby that said NO PETS, and got them both inside her door before anyone was the wiser.

She put on some rock 'n' roll in case that nosy jerk across the hall was listening, and gave the dog a good long bath with her best Paul Mitchell shampoo. She didn't have any dog food, but she had some hamburger, so she cooked up a few burgers.

She ate one and the dog ate three. She had never seen a hamburger disappear so quickly. She got into bed and watched an old Katharine Hepburn movie, and when the dog climbed up with her, circled three times and plopped down at her side, she didn't object. It felt good to be needed.

u u u

In the morning Brenda remembered why she had never owned a dog. A dog has to be walked. Brenda didn't much like to walk. But a few minutes before 6 o'clock the dog was at her door, snuffling at it and scratching a little bit. Brenda signed, got up, put her sweats on, cut six feet from the ball of twine she used for packages, looped it around the dog's neck, and out they went.

The sky was a color Brenda thought she had never seen before, a kind of pale blue that seemed to get bluer and more intense as they walked. She realized that she generally stayed in until she had to leave for work at 8:22 every morning – she had never been out this early. It was weird, that sky. It was also kind of beautiful.

They had gone 20 blocks when Brenda started thinking about coffee. She wanted coffee. She needed her coffee. They found a Tim Hortons and walked up to the drive-thru window. You can't take dogs into Tim Hortons.

"Coffee, please. Large."

"Anything else?"

Brenda looked down at the dog. She could see his ribs sticking out.

"A box of Timbits."

They sat on the bench in a little park that she had never noticed, and she fed the dog two dozen doughnut holes, one by one. It took about 30 seconds. Then she untied the twine and the dog chased squirrels and barked at the cars, and Brenda sat and watched him and drank her coffee. Good coffee, she thought. Hot and strong and black. She breathed in the city air. It tasted sweet.

♦ ♦ ♦

Later that day they went to the dog park. There were benches there for the people to sit on while the dogs played, but Brenda didn't sit. She threw a Frisbee for the dog, and then he went and played with the other dogs and she talked to some people who were doing the same thing, watching their dogs and talking about dogs and about life in the city and about the things they wanted to do, the new restaurants they had heard about and the jobs they were hoping to get and the discussion groups they were in at their church. Somebody asked her dog's name, and she said it was Tim. She told this one woman that she was a paralegal, and the woman was really interested and asked her all about it. The dogs chased each other until their tongues hung out the side of their mouth. The people chattered away as if the world were their oyster. Brenda had never seen so much energy. She stopped and bought a proper collar and leash, and she and Tim ran all the way home.

♦ ♦ ♦

Thursday night, Brenda was making a special dinner for the two of them, her and Tim, when the phone rang. It was the woman she had met at the dog park. It seems there was a kind of supper club that some of the dog-park people went to. The people ate potluck and the dogs ate each other's dog food for a special treat. Would she

{ 22 }

like to come?

Sure. But her fridge was pretty empty, and so was her purse. She decided she'd just get some fancy bread to take to the party. There was a bakery she had noticed, so she and Tim went there and she told the baker about the party, and did he have any fancy party bread she could take?

The baker laughed a little and produced two enormous loaves of pain de campagne, so beautiful they were like little works of art. "Two dollars," he said. "I love dogs, too." She paid him and he wrapped up the bread. Brenda noticed that Tim was off in a corner of the bakery, looking up at something on the counter. She saw the yellow box before she knew what it was: a box of Timbits.

The baker was a little sheepish. "Customer must have left those there," he muttered. Tim barked a high-pitched bark. He wagged his tail hard. The baker looked at him.

Brenda and Tim both got their daily bread that day.

• • •

She had never seen so much food. People had brought casseroles; they had brought fancy appetizers involving toothpicks; there were complicated little sushi things and fresh fruit and pies for dessert, and good red wine to drink and kids underfoot. They had the party outside, in somebody's big fenced yard, and the dogs ran around like crazy and ate each other's food and had to be chased away from the people food. Everybody hugged everybody, even people they didn't know, and everybody ate until they felt like one more bite would put them over the edge.

Brenda hadn't felt so alive in years. She talked to everybody and ate herself silly. Tim ran in circles, he was so excited, and he ate Alpo and Kennel Ration and Purina Dog Chow, and he made everybody laugh when he came and begged for the one little box of Timbits on the dessert table. There was noise and laughter and things got spilled and the dogs licked them up, and by the time it was over, Brenda knew she had found some kind of kindred spirits here. It wasn't about the dogs or the food or any of that. It just was … right somehow, that these people had shown up in her life just at this time, in this city, under a rising moon bigger than she had ever seen.

She got a ride home from a guy she had met at the party, who worked for a nonprofit organization that helped poor people who were having trouble with their landlords, and women who were trying to get away from their abusive husbands. He took the long way to her apartment, but she didn't mind, because they were talking about the law and how it really matters when you can use it to help people, and the things that he did with this agency and the way they always needed good people to help with the work. Tim and the other dog were in the back seat. They had finished sniffing each other and now they were hanging their heads out the windows, laughing the way dogs do with their black lips flapping in the wind, the strong wind rich with all the subtle smells of the world. The car drove up along a little ridge overlooking the city. Brenda had never seen the lights of the city at night from up above like this, and maybe it was the good red wine, but they seemed to shimmer like jewels in her eyes. It was all she could do to keep from crying.

They woke up the next morning, Brenda and Tim, just before 6, like always. Actually, this time Brenda woke up first. Her mind was racing with possibilities. She got dressed and slipped the collar on the dog while he was still sprawled out on the bed. *Her* dog.

The sun was just starting to warm up the morning. The city was just beginning to stir. A long day stretched ahead.

She got the leash and hooked him up. "Up and at 'em, Tim," she said. "C'mon, boy. Let's go see what the world has to offer."

What the Sky Said

M a t t h e w   2 : 1 - 6

Everyone knew that Megan was a scientist. For one thing, she told them all the time. "I am a scientist," she said, to whoever would listen. And even though she had just turned ten years old, they believed her.

For one thing, she spent hours with her chemistry set, trying to figure out why some chemicals made smoke when you mixed them and some didn't. She could already write programs for her mom's computer. Her favorite was one that played a Miley Cyrus song when her mom went on the Tom Petty Web site. Megan's mom couldn't stand Miley Cyrus, and she never figured out that it was Megan who had played that trick on her.

Most of all, everyone knew Megan was a scientist because they saw her outside at night, in all kinds of weather, looking at the sky with her telescope. Megan had to buy it herself, because since her father died they didn't have much money. So she collected pop cans, 7,249 of them, and turned them in at the Shop-Rite until she had enough money. It took her two years. But Megan was a scientist. Scientists are patient.

Her telescope was the best thing she had ever owned. It was a Starmaster 2000, and it had tripod legs and an easy-focus eyepiece and a really strong lens. On a clear night, she could even see Neptune. But the best thing about this telescope was that up on top was a digital camera that could take a picture of whatever you were seeing. Once Megan took a picture of Mars that was so pretty, her teacher hung it in the science lab.

This is a story of what Megan saw one Christmas Eve through her telescope.

Her mom didn't really want her to be out in the back yard that night. Who goes stargazing on Christmas Eve, after all? Shouldn't she be inside leaving cookies for Santa Claus and looking at the lights on the tree and getting her pajamas on?

But they got home early from the church service, and Megan had a good nap during the sermon, so she had all sorts of energy and there was no way she was going to sleep any time soon. Plus her brother had been bugging her, the way little brothers do, and her mom was kind of cranky from all the overtime she had been putting in at work.

A scientist knows when the time is right. Megan put on her cutest pouty face and said, "Pleeeeease?"

"It's freezing out there, Megan. Can't you do it another night?"

"That means it's just right, Mom. It's too cold to snow, so there's no clouds. And it's a new moon, so it's a nice dark sky. I want to look for that comet I heard about on the news."

"You're probably looking for Santa," her brother piped up. "Take his picture for me, huh?"

Megan gritted her teeth. How could she be expected to be nice when her brother was always so naughty?

"All right." Her mother gave a little sigh. "An hour, no more. And bundle up!"

Megan was already heading outside. It was quiet out there; no cars, no TV, just the crunch of her boots on the snow. She got the telescope from its place in the garage and set it up on its three legs. She tilted the barrel skyward. East-northeast, that's what they had said about the comet. But they weren't sure if it would be visible. She looked through the eyepiece, trying to find some sign.

To tell the truth, she thought, she could use a sign. Things were so much different now that her father was gone. Nobody smiled much anymore, especially her mom. It was like there was a big hole in the middle of their lives.

The minister had said that love never really dies, that God never leaves us even when we lose people we love, that God sent Jesus to show us that he knows what it means to be human. What it means to hurt sometimes.

But Megan was a scientist. She needed proof. That church stuff was OK if you believed it, but she wasn't sure. She never said this to anyone, but sometimes she thought that if God was really there and really loved us, people wouldn't cry so much. It was hard to know for sure.

And when her aunt took her aside after the funeral and assured her that Daddy was in heaven and there was nothing to be afraid of, well, the scientist had a hard time with that one, too. Because Megan had a Starmaster 2000. She looked at the heavens a lot. And she saw stars and planets and even a comet once in a while, but they were what they were and only that. It wasn't like they pointed to anything. She wanted proof. She wanted to know for sure.

No comet. Those TV guys didn't know the sky, anyway. They were always getting it wrong.

But out of the corner of her eye she saw something else. A shooting star.

She had seen shooting stars before, and she knew all about them. They were space junk, really, just little pieces of rock that bumped into the atmosphere really fast and burned up just as fast. But they were kind of neat, because you could watch for a long time and never be quite sure when the next one was coming.

Megan turned her telescope east, toward where she had seen the streak of light in the sky. She thought she'd try an experiment: Was she fast enough to take a picture of a shooting star? She held the shutter release in her hand and watched. There! A streak of light, like some supersonic firefly. She pushed the button – *click*. She could upload these pictures onto the computer later, see if she had gotten lucky. They were so fast, it was hard to know whether she had her shooting-star picture.

There! Another one. *Click.* And again. And again. Megan clicked away, and the shooting stars were coming faster now, maybe every ten seconds. There was something strange, though. Usually shooting stars went right to left, and some of these did, but a lot of them were coming straight down, like a light bulb falling out of the sky. Weird. Megan had never seen that. She kept taking pictures.

Click. Click. Click.

"Megan!" Her mother's voice. "C'mon inside. It's freezing."

"I'll be right there." *Click. Click. Click.*

"Now!"

The telescope camera had a memory card; you took it out and plugged it into the computer. Megan put the card into her pocket and put the telescope back in the garage.

Her brother was already in bed. Her mom had made cocoa, and Megan warmed her hands around the steaming mug. She headed for the computer. Her mother tagged along. Megan knew she was lonely. It was the first Christmas since her dad had died.

Megan plugged in the memory card and booted up the photo program. She must have taken a hundred pictures. She was sure to have a shooting star in there somewhere.

She clicked on "Load Photos." The machine whirred and grumbled, and then an icon appeared on the screen. One.

"Oh, no!"

"What's the matter?" her mom asked.

"I thought I had like fifty pictures. There's only one! I must have set it wrong. I bet the first time I clicked the shutter, it just stayed open. It's been staring at the sky for an hour!"

"So is there a picture?" her mom asked.

"Just one. It's probably nothing. It's probably ruined," the scientist said.

She clicked on the icon. A picture filled the screen. Megan and her mom stared at it.

Over and over, the camera had captured the image of the heavenly lights.

The sky was black black black. But there in front of them were the delicate white trails of a hundred shooting stars – some of them going left to right, some of them going up and down.

A simple, perfect cross, written in light on the sky.

Now, a scientist doesn't take things on faith. She needs evidence. She needs proof. But that Christmas Eve, as Megan and her mother sat looking at that cross made of light, they cried. Their tears were not those of the grief they shared. They were the tears of a truth that goes deeper than knowledge. There was a hole in the middle of their family, and that would never change. But in the sky that night, written in the cool white light of the heavens, came a sign of hope: hope as big as the universe, as joyful as birth and as deep as forever. And that Christmas Eve, Megan the scientist received her greatest gift: a glimpse of the unseen, the assurance that God is near, the evidence of hope for a family set adrift and for a world gone astray.

The Ride

P s a l m   2 3

J o h n   1 0 : 2 2 - 3 0

It was late afternoon before Leo got the last of the boxes unloaded at the frozen-food terminal in Dubuque and gunned the tractor-trailer onto Iowa Route 151, headed toward Cedar Rapids. He'd had enough of the interstate for today, he decided. Seventy-five miles and he'd have the big rig back in its bay; five miles more and he'd be at home with a Rolling Rock in one hand and the remote in the other. The first of several Rolling Rocks, he admitted as much. Well, he drove hard all day; drinking hard seemed like poetic justice.

Had to watch for deer, though. You never knew when one would come leaping out of the scrubby brush ten feet from the road's edge. Or two – they seemed to travel in pairs. One panicky twist of the wheel and he could be in the ditch, or worse.

He was scanning the roadside, watching for movement, when a tiny figure appeared on the shoulder up ahead. Couldn't be a person, he thought. Not in this heat. But as he rumbled closer, he saw the figure more clearly – a boy maybe ten years old, in faded blue jeans and basketball sneakers and a ludicrous muscle shirt, not hitch-hiking but looking balefully into the eyes of the drivers. Leo's eyes.

Why did he stop? Thinking it over that night, he tried to explain it to himself. Maybe the kid needed help. Maybe he was lost. He looked hot, and the A/C in the cab was cranked full blast. Or maybe, Leo conceded to himself, both of them were a little lost on that desolate stretch of highway. It wouldn't hurt to have someone to talk to.

◆ ◆ ◆

The boy slung a little backpack into the cab, climbed in and shut the door. He smelled of parched earth, and his dirty hair was the color of cornstalks.

"Got any Co-Cola?"

Leo was taken aback. "Where are you heading?"

"Cedar Rapids, but I'm not picky about it. I'll go where you're going. I'm only going home."

Leo got the truck back up to cruising speed. "Put that seat belt on, huh? And yeah, there are some Cokes in that little cooler there. Help yourself."

The boy drained the can in three gulps, then settled against the window and surrendered himself to the hypnotism of the passing farmland. The drone of the engine washed over him like an anesthetic. It was a feeling that Leo knew all too well – road-weariness, friend of the passenger but enemy of the driver. The boy's utter ease unsettled him. He was afraid of falling into that trap.

"Why are you out here in the middle of nowhere?"

"You sound like my mom," the boy answered promptly.

"It just seemed like not much fun."

"Uh-huh. But it's quiet out here. It's not quiet in Cedar Rapids. I got a ride from these people in a big black car, but they were turning off, I got out back there. I been looking for rocks. I collect them – heart-shaped rocks."

"Why?"

"Why what?"

"Why collect heart-shaped rocks?"

"They make me happy," the boy said. "Like, there's a million billion rocks in the world, right? But there's only a few that *mean* something. Those are the ones I'm looking for."

"What do they mean?" Leo asked. He wanted to know.

The boy paused. Leo could see a moment of indecision, a question of whether to trust. Behind his eyes, something shifted.

"Didn't you ever get a valentine, mister? Heart means love. Lots of people throw rocks; I line 'em up on my shelf. They make me happy."

Leo was silent. Happiness was a concept he had pushed to the back of his mind for a long time now, since Carol died. They had been happy together, but it was something Leo never thought about while she was alive. Never once. But when he walked into that empty house after the funeral service, a house where the smell of her cologne still lingered in the closets and the kitchen bore the marks of her paintbrush, he felt the bottom of his stomach fall into oblivion. A cruel trick, he thought – he knew he had been happy only when the whole deal disappeared.

The blacktop shimmered dreamily with the rising heat. Snap out of it, he told himself. Push it back. You're doing fine.

The boy was down on the floor of the passenger side, fooling around with his backpack, taking something out of it. He climbed back into the seat, his hands making a sphere around some secret.

"What's that?"

"Promise you won't throw me out?"

Leo grunted noncommittally, and the boy took it as a yes.

"It's a chameleon. Look, I found him under a rock next to a falling-down barn. It was damp down there. They like it kind of wet, and there hasn't been much rain. But he liked it down there."

Leo looked at the little lizard peeking out between the boy's interlaced fingers. Its tail stuck out below, curled up like a cinnamon bun. The chameleon looked at him glassily.

"What does it eat?"

"Bugs, mostly. I read about them in this book I have about lizards. I saw him eat a fly."

"Well, I don't think I have any bugs in here." Leo thought for a moment. "There's a cheese sandwich in that cooler. Does he like cheese?"

"I dunno. Let me try." The boy got the sandwich, pinched off a speck of cheese the size of a thumbtack, and put it in front of the chameleon's nose. The chameleon gobbled it down.

"Cool." The boy got himself another Coke and ate the sandwich. He put the chameleon on the driver's log on the dashboard, and while the boy ate, the animal faded from bright green to the pale beige of a manila folder.

"He does that a lot," the boy said. "Changes color, I mean. It's so birds won't eat him. It's like he's part of whatever he's sitting on. It's like he disappears."

Despite himself, Leo was intrigued. "Why doesn't he just run away from the birds?"

"He's so small," the boy said, "and the birds are so big, and they watch from the sky. He needs to hide. He's afraid."

"But what if the bird eats plants?"

The boy frowned. "Birds don't eat plants," he said pointedly. "He's safe. He disappears."

Leo let it drop. There was a sullen edge to the boy's voice. They traveled in silence toward the sinking sun, already turning orange across the Great Plains. The odometer rolled up the miles, a trucker's time clock ticking away.

• • •

"Where's the farthest you ever drove?" the boy said out of a dead silence. Leo had thought he was asleep.

"I've driven out west some. California. Nevada. I went through Death Valley once."

"What's that?"

"This big canyon, like nothing here in Iowa. It's all desert, big rock formations, mountains all around. You get down in there and it's like being in a closet with your furnace. A hundred and thirty degrees sometimes."

"Why's it called Death Valley?"

"Well, you were out there walking around in ninety degrees. How long do you figure you could do that for?"

"I dunno."

"Not forever. You need water; you need an idea of where you're going. If you're all alone, you're not going to make it. In Death Valley, that's it times a hundred. People get lost there and never come back. When they find them, it's just nice white bones."

Immediately he regretted saying it.

"Jeez." A pause. "Did you get lost?"

"I had a map and a compass and water and a cell phone. I needed to get back home. I called my wife right in the middle of it."

"Were you afraid?"

Leo considered. "It's an evil place, but I wasn't afraid. I knew I could count on myself, count on this truck, to get me out of there."

The boy thought about that. The landscape kept passing by. On the dashboard, the chameleon was lying in the sun. You could hardly see it against the manila folder.

"I have to pee."

Leo sighed. That was always the way it was with kids. Or so he had heard; never had any of his own.

"Can't you wait? We're not that far from Cedar Rapids."

"I have to pee *now*."

Leo negotiated the big rig onto the shoulder but left it running. The sun was low, and he hated driving in the dark. The boy opened the door, climbed down, trotted toward a little rise and disappeared behind it.

"Hurry it up," Leo said, only half out loud.

A minute passed. Two. Three. Five. "C'mon," Leo thought. "Let's go, kid."

Still no boy.

Leo turned off the ignition and stepped out. It felt good to stretch his legs, his back. Driving takes a toll.

He climbed up over the rise and saw the boy a hundred yards farther on, crouched, not moving. Leo walked briskly toward him, half in exasperation and half in worry.

When they were in whispering distance, the boy looked back. "Shhhhhh!" he said.

Leo slowed down, stepped gingerly. He got to the boy's side and the boy pointed. Not ten feet away, in magnificent profile, was a ring-necked pheasant the size of a basketball. Leo looked at it. The bird was strutting, bobbing its head the way birds do. A shock of white made a circle around its throat. There was a splash of red on its face. Heart-shaped red.

"I saw him come out of those trees there," the boy whispered. "I followed him."

There was an old stump; Leo sat. The boy knelt on the matted grass beside him. They watched the pheasant for a while, framed in the hot oranges and reds of the setting sun. Leo couldn't take his eyes off the bird. In the parched earth tones of this godforsaken field, here was a creature with colors as bright as a construction cone. He went back to the truck and got them some Cokes, and they sat and drank them and watched some more.

♦ ♦ ♦

When they got to where the boy needed to go, the daylight was just starting to give way to starlight. The boy lived at the far end of a long dirt driveway. Leo stopped the truck on the road.

"Thanks for those Co-Colas." The boy gathered up his backpack.

"You got that lizard?" He did. "You going to be OK?"

The boy had his feet on the ground. "I was gonna ask you the same thing."

"I'll be fine," said Leo. "Fine."

The boy started down the driveway.

Leo wrestled the double-clutch into gear, and the rig edged into motion. He was three houses down when he looked in the rearview in spite of himself. The boy had come back to the road and was watching the truck pull away. His hands were cupped in front of him, holding the chameleon with the gentleness of a father. His face was a question. His eyes seemed far away.

Multiple Choice

H e b r e w s   4 : 1 2

1   T h e s s a l o n i a n s   2 : 1 3

Fourth grade, Miss Phillips' class. Miss Phillips, famous for scowling at them that fifth grade was going to be so much tougher and they had better get their act together, because they couldn't stay in fourth grade forever and life is difficult.

Julie stands when she hears her name. Stands up fast, because she has been day-dreaming. Tries to get her bearings.

Miss Phillips repeats the question, from last night's chapter of the book they are supposed to be reading: "Why do you think Anne left the farm?" Julie doesn't know. She spent last night watching TV. She tries to improvise, but fear has her brain in lockdown. She opens her mouth but nothing comes out.

"Sit down, Julie." Miss Phillips gives her that legendary glare. Julie sits. She feels hot and red; she can hear the others snickering. The teacher moves on to another victim, but right then and there Julie makes herself a promise. She will be a woman of the book. Never again will she be caught answerless. Defenseless. She will start to read.

Fast-forward ... further ... a little further ... there.

It's morning rounds at the hospital where Julie is an intern. She is a doctor and she still can't get used to the idea – the "M.D." on the name tag she wears on her white lab coat, the way people step aside when she walks down the hall. She is a doctor, but still a student. Another year of apprenticeship stretches ahead, Julie and a half-dozen others trailing around after the older docs and supposedly learning what they need to know to be real doctors.

Julie doesn't need this, she knows. She is a woman of the book. Where the others groused and fought it, Julie loved the intricacies of med school. Especially she loved the books, lavishly illustrated tours of the human body with sentences like "Oriented obliquely, the major fissure extends posteriorly and superiorly approximately to the level of the fourth vertebral body."

In rounds she delights in the diagnostic routine, ticking off the symptoms on a patient's chart – "chest pain, numbness right hand, chills, slight jaundice" – and computing them back to a textbook answer. She spends her nights reviewing her anatomy texts, to make sure she has it right. She is rewarded for it, too. The other interns have learned to look to her when the attending physician asks the question. They know she's got it.

But today it's only her and the on-call doc. One-on-ones, they call it – one experienced physician, one ready to learn, and a unit full of lessons.

It's almost 9 at night when they reach the last one.

"233A," Julie recites. "Female, age 71, came in Thursday with gastrointestinal complaints of unknown origin, otherwise a clean history. BP a little elevated. That's about it."

The attending, Dr. Ramos, looks at the chart and they go in.

"Good evening, Mrs. Jankowski," he says quietly. The patient is curled up in bed, motionless. Above them the frantic light show of the TV plays out soundlessly. "How are you feeling?"

Mrs. Jankowski stirs and looks without comprehension.

"I am Dr. Ramos, and this is Dr. Jordan. Do you mind if we examine you?"

The patient nods and pulls back the covers. The hospital gown is loose on her frail body. Dr. Ramos listens to her abdomen with a stethoscope, and so does Julie. They do the usual song-and-dance: cough, breathe, turn. Does this hurt? Does that?

"Will you excuse us for a minute?" Dr. Ramos says to the patient. He takes Julie back out into the hall. "What do you see?"

"Abdomen sounds good. I don't see any evidence of sepsis. Vitals are fine. As far as I can see, she shouldn't be here."

Dr. Ramos frowns. "And yet here she is, and she is hurting." He looks again at the chart. "Did you do the intake on this woman?"

"Yes."

He frowns again, and motions her back into the room.

"Mrs. Jankowski," he begins. "Do you mind if we sit down?"

"Suit yourself."

They sit. Dr. Ramos takes the patient's hand.

"Mrs. Jankowski," he says, "tell me your story."

She looks at him suspiciously. "What do you mean?"

"Where have you been in your life? What's the best thing that ever happened to you? What's the worst? Who are the people who are important to you? How has life treated you?"

Julie watches in confusion. Where is this going? She tries to remember this method from her books on bedside procedures, but it's not there. She feels lost.

Mrs. Jankowski turns toward Dr. Ramos. She sits up and draws the blanket to her.

"For example," Dr. Ramos says, "tell me about those numbers."

Julie hadn't noticed them. Four faint blue digits on her left wrist.

"It was in 1943," Mrs. Jankowski says. "They came when we were sleeping, my brother and me. The knock on the door woke me. They loaded us into trucks. The children were in one truck, the grown-ups were in another. They took the children first. My brother tried to fight, but they were so strong. My mother watched from the doorway. They said we would be together again, the soldiers did, but that was a lie. A lie. We never saw my mother and father again. They died at Dachau. I have seen their names on the list."

The room seems very small. Julie watches; Dr. Ramos is intent on the patient's face. She keeps talking.

"My brother and I came to America a few years later. After it was all over. It was hard, but we had been through hard. He went to Chicago – we have cousins there – but when I married Walter, I came here. It has been a good life. We were happy."

Mrs. Jankowski is behind blank eyes. Memories have overtaken her. Julie starts to speak, to break the silence, but checks herself. They sit there, three human beings, in a sacred space.

"Mrs. Jankowski?" Dr. Ramos takes her hand again. "You have told us much. What else do you want to say?"

His voice brings her back to this room, to her bed, to her complaining stomach. Julie can see tears gathering in her eyes.

"He was good to me," the woman says. "Walter. We had to bury him proper. Even though it was winter and the ground was hard. Even though it was more than I really could afford. He was a good husband. Forty-eight years we had together." The tears are in tendrils down her weathered face. "I hope he's not cold. I hope he's all right."

Fast-forward, but only a little. Hospital cafeteria, midnight. Dr. Ramos is buying. They sit in contemplative silence in the overbright room. Julie pours sugar into the brackish hospital coffee.

"How did you know?" she asks.

"I didn't," he says. "You never know. You can only open up a space to hear."

"So what happens now?"

"She'll be fine," Dr. Ramos says. "Or as fine as a person can be who has been part of something for forty-eight years and suddenly finds herself not part of that something."

"But what do we do about her gastrointestinal complaint?"

"There isn't much we can do. Medically, that is. Maybe a scrip for Zantac or something like that, keep the acids down. But I think we might have done her some good. You have to remember that sometimes there has to be healing before we can talk about a cure."

Julie looks at him quizzically.

"Healing," Dr. Ramos says. "I would bet you a doughnut that she hasn't spoken of her childhood for decades. And I'd bet you another that she hasn't cried all of her tears over her husband's death. The body will heal itself. That's one thing you need to remember, doctor. We can correct things that go wrong – sometimes we can, anyway – but we can't always fix things for these people. We can cure. Healing, that comes from somewhere else. She'll have to find her own way there."

"That's not good enough," Julie says. "I want her to be better. I want them all to be better. Otherwise, why even bother? I put in all this work – all the reading, all the studying, all that school – and you're telling me I'm not a healer?"

Dr. Ramos looks at her evenly, the teacher calculating his strategy. He stirs his coffee. Finally he makes a decision.

"Julie," he says, "tell me your story."

Dinner for Two

1 Corinthians 11 : 23 - 26

Stupid foreign cars, McMillan thought to himself as the Renault sped through the French countryside. If they built them any smaller, the trunk would be in the front bumper.

From the passenger seat, Linda could see the sourness play across his face. This was not the easiest assignment she had ever had, she thought wryly. Sure, it sounded glamorous – personal assistant to the great food writer Rex McMillan, accompanying him to Paris for the meal to end all meals. But she had learned quickly that McMillan brought to his job, and his life, a temperament that he shared with some of the world's best chefs: a churlish impatience with anything short of excellence, and that included people.

Now, as they hurtled west through the darkness along the A13, she tried to break the uneasy silence with McMillan's favorite topic.

"So how was it?" she asked.

She knew he had to write the story soon, and thought talking it through might help him. The assignment was simple: Take an unlimited expense account, make some plans with the best restaurant in the world's best restaurant city, Paris, and enjoy the finest meal ever made. She had watched as McMillan held court in a private room of the Chez Henri, where it seemed like no one got out the door without dropping three hundred dollars.

But that was pocket change, in this experiment. She watched as the food writer nibbled and sampled his way through a delicate appetizer of prawns in a brandy sauce, a salad featuring greens flown in from Colombia and Laos, a beef bourguignon for which the cow had been specially raised, a soup of leeks and truffles and some kind of scarce mushroom that was hand-gathered in the remote hills of India. McMillan ate it all without comment, stopping only to make some cutting remark to the one person he allowed to join him, a venerated French wine writer who seemed to be McMillan's only friend.

Linda, of course, wasn't at the table. The kitchen staff had slipped her a green salad, which she ate quickly in case McMillan needed her attention. There was no charge for the salad. They gave Linda the bill for the big dinner, and it wasn't until they were safely outside Chez Henri that she dared to look at it. It was in euros, but she did the math: three thousand, seven hundred dollars. Dinner for two.

That was seven hours ago. He had taken his dinner at noon, in the European way. Now she was feeling the pangs of hunger again, and with McMillan's legendary appetite, she suspected he was hungry too.

"The meal," she said again. "How was it?"

McMillan scowled. "I've had better," he said. "I'm not kidding. The beef was a little tough; you'd think with all that wine it would have loosened up some. And those prawns! They must have been three days old. If the chef thinks he can fool me with a refrigerator, he's got another thing coming."

"How are you going to write it?" she asked.

McMillan leveled his gaze at her. To be stuck with such an assistant, and four more days on the road through French wine country with her. He would have to speak to the editor about this injustice.

"I will," he pronounced, "write the truth."

They rode in silence for a while. The road was dark and narrow and without guardrails, and on both sides it dropped off into blackness. McMillan drove fast, hoping, Linda saw, to get to Le Havre soon for supper at a place he had mentioned before. Like most men, she thought, he got irritable when he was hungry.

"Is there any radio this far out?" he said. She reached for the Renault's overcomplicated radio, the good assistant, but his hand was already there. He frowned at the buttons, punching them one by one and hearing only hiss.

She heard gravel under the tires. McMillan jerked his head up, and the steering wheel swung violently to the right. She heard herself scream, and then everything went black.

• • •

"Bloody hell," McMillan was saying. Linda felt herself swimming back to consciousness as if from the bottom of a well. Something was pressed against her legs, immobilizing them; it hurt, but not unbearably. Otherwise, unbelievably, she was uninjured.

Out the window she could see a stone wall high above them; the rest was blackness. They were in a deep ditch.

She looked over at McMillan, afraid of what she'd see. The writer was twisted sideways, and the steering column had been forced into the cabin, pinning him against the battered driver's-side door. A three-inch gash on his forehead was bleeding profusely.

"Bloody hell," he said again. Then: "Are you all right?"

"I think so," Linda said. "What happened?"

"Tire must have caught on the embankment. Flipped us right around, down and around. Can you get out?"

"No."

"Me either. Bloody hell."

She found a wad of tissues in her purse and reached toward him.

"Ow!"

"Just hold this on your forehead. It'll stop the bleeding."

He did it. And so there they were, strangers in a strange land, sharing a few cubic feet of living space. And maybe, she thought, dying space.

"Do you see any lights?"

She didn't.

"Me either. Would be nice if there were a farmhouse around, wouldn't it? Can't count on the French for anything." He paused. "Not much traffic on this road, either. I can't remember seeing any other cars for a couple hours at least, when we were driving."

"It's the main road to Le Havre," Linda said. "Seems like somebody would be driving it."

"It's almost 10. They pride themselves on early-to-bed, early-to-rise. No wonder Benjamin Franklin was ambassador to France."

They sat in silence for a long time.

"Heck of a trip for you, isn't it?"

McMillan's question startled her. It was the first time he had noticed her, an actual person and not just his assistant. She looked over at him.

"Well, it wasn't what I bargained for. But it's been kind of an adventure."

McMillan smiled. She hadn't seen that before. "They say it's when you're safe at home that you wish you were having an adventure. But when you're actually on an adventure, that's when you wish you were safe at home."

"Eternal discontent," Linda said. "So what about you? Do you wish you were safe at home?"

McMillan pondered. "Well, I'm trapped in a lousy car, in the dark, in a country I despise; I'm hungry and I've got a story to write, and God knows if we're ever going to get out of this. My adventures should come at the table."

"So: safe at home?"

"In New York, that's a contradiction in terms. But we'll get there. Somebody will come along eventually." He pushed at the steering wheel; the horn sounded. "We'll signal them."

More silence. Outside, the wind rustled through grapevines and heather.

"Do you mind if I ask you something?" Linda said. "You write about food, but you don't seem to enjoy it all that much. So why do you do it?"

McMillan smiled. He dabbed at his bloody forehead with the tissues. "Seems kind of silly at this point, doesn't it?" he said. "A four thousand dollar dinner, and here we are paying the price. I guess I don't know how to answer you. There should be pleasures in life, but there should also be depth to those pleasures, some meaning behind them. Otherwise we live and die and haven't touched anything eternal. There's something elemental about food. I just keep hoping to find that taste of the eternal. I haven't found it yet."

Linda let that sink in.

"And to tell you the truth, I'm so hungry right now, I've forgotten dinner entirely."

At Chez Henri, the kitchen steward had pulled Linda aside and pressed into her hand a paper bag. "Take this," he had said. "For you. For you to enjoy."

Now Linda rooted behind her in the back seat until she found the bag. "Maybe this will do," she said, and pulled out its contents:

A crusty loaf of bread. A wheel of Camembert. An elegant cheese knife. And two tiny bottles of Bordeaux, of an excellent vintage.

McMillan's eyes widened, but he said nothing.

Linda spread out the bag between them. She broke the bread and gave him half. She unwrapped the cheese and stuck the knife into it. McMillan opened the wine and sniffed at it.

They clinked the little bottles in a wordless toast, and drank. And there in the ruined car, swallowed in darkness, thrown together as strangers with a common hunger, they ate. They tore hunks off the loaf with their fingers and spread the delicate cheese on it, and they ate with such simple joy that heaven and earth seemed to distill itself into this one meal. The night loomed long, and they were hurting and were strangers to this place, but they ate and drank, and it was good. It was astonishingly good.

In the distance lights rose, and it was impossible to tell whether they were headlights or the coming of the dawn.

Runner's High

1 C O R I N T H I A N S   1 4 : 1 5

In January it was the hardest, she had decided. Supposedly the days were getting longer, but outside the deep freeze seemed like it would never end. The darkness hung like a heavy curtain in the air, and when the alarm called her out of the other world, called her back to this world with its demands and its relentless logic, she couldn't help but groan.

She had fought this fight before, of course, hundreds of times now. Her solution was a solitary minute of laziness, nestled under the covers while she watched for the clock to turn over. Then 7:01 flashed red, and she forced herself out of bed. She put on three layers – Lycra, cotton, then nylon for a windbreak; laced up the expensive shoes that were a Christmas treat; and opened the front door. Time to run.

It had been like this every morning for going on two years now: the mental struggle, the climb out of bed, those first stiff steps as she hit the road. But there was no other way. She would never go back to where she had been, pushing two hundred pounds and hating it. Now she had imposed upon herself a strict discipline of diet and exercise, and it had paid off. She was a shadow of her former self; there in the pre-dawn darkness, she smiled at the idea. No shadows here. Just the steady slip of her Nikes along the city streets, the white puffs of her breath, the imagined protests of her heart as it began to beat harder.

Five miles. A distance with its own arc of exertion and emotion.

She turned down Central Avenue and considered the tightness in her calves. They seemed to be weighing her down, as if she were lugging rolls of quarters in her socks. Her shoulders, too – tight, not yet feeling the blood.

She ran anyway.

Some people said they did their best thinking on a run like this. She could never understand that. There was too much to manage with the body to have much left over for the brain. She loosened the drawstring of her hooded sweatshirt to let a little air in. She could feel her core body temperature start to come up, feel the warmth in her torso, feel it radiate into her head.

But the legs were still tight. She felt graceless. Her breath was labored.

She remembered those first runs, two years ago. When the trainer had suggested she hit the track, she almost laughed. She couldn't possibly, she thought. At first she walked – one lap, then two, then more. The first time she walked a mile, she smiled the whole rest of the day. A whole mile! She imagined standing on the Thruway and looking at the distance markers. Even on the straight stretches, a mile was too far to see. And she had walked one.

Then she tried to run, and it was different. Harder on the knees; harder on the lungs. The first time she tried it, tried a half-mile at a pace that little kids routinely ran in races, she couldn't do it. She had to stop and lean against the goalposts, and, she was ashamed to admit, she cried a little bit.

But she was finding a resolve she didn't recognize. The next day she tried again, and the next, and within a few weeks she was trotting her four laps doggedly, if not happily. The weight was starting to come off, and she figured it was worth the pain.

She turned now toward the park, into her second mile in the early morning cold. One long circuit here, the biggest part of the run. She never loosened up in those early days, she remembered. No wonder it was so painful. Now she could feel her muscles lengthening as the warmth spread through her body. It was a kind of magic she had come to expect and to love – that moment when the experience transformed itself from awkward struggle to fluid motion. She hopped over a puddle and clapped her gloved hands. The air felt good. She had begun to glide.

Her trainer had talked a lot about strength. "Pain is weakness leaving the body," he had said over and over. That made her mad. She had spent her life trying to avoid pain. When she hurt, when others hurt her, she smoothed it over with ice cream and mashed potatoes and isolation. Rough edges seemed to hurt her more than they did other people. But she paid for it with a body that started to seem alien to her, as if she were living in a cocoon. But cocoons break open and something beautiful emerges. This one just stayed in place, protecting her but also squeezing the life out of her. In the worst times, she felt as if she couldn't breathe.

The cocoon was still there. She knew she would never be one of those people who felt things lightly, and so she would always have to guard against the temptation to wrap herself in unhealthy comfort. But as the pounds fell away, so did the idea that criticism, or failure, or rejection, would kill her. She found herself speaking in public more, making plans rather than reacting to things, cultivating friendships. Sometimes things hurt, but five miles every morning worked that hurt through her muscles and breathed it out her lungs.

Pain leaving the body. She had found her strength.

She rounded the far side of the park and began the journey back. A few other runners were out, lost in their own internal soliloquies. She nodded to them as they passed; they nodded back; that was all. She had tried running with friends; it was safer that way, for one thing. But they wanted to talk to pass the time, and finally she decided she couldn't bear it. She didn't run for distraction. She ran for catharsis – to empty herself, to reconnect with something she was searching for, to get back in touch with her body, to refill herself for the day.

Three miles done. Downhill from here.

Not literally, of course. That would be too easy. She had read about people who had tried to become better runners through mind control. If you *think* downhill, they said, you'll *feel* downhill. It gets easier. If you think gravity is your friend, it won't hurt so much.

She had tried it, but of course it didn't work. There were some things that were impossible to deny, and gravity was one of those things.

What worked better for her was what she was starting to feel now, as her shoes slipped along the pavement and the reluctant gray light of a winter dawn began to show itself. And it worked because it was her reward – her Cracker Jack surprise for the two years she had strained to get to this point, and the everyday struggle to overcome her inertia, get onto the road, and run through the stiffness until she started to feel graceful and fluid and alive again.

What worked was the rhythm of the whole thing. A lot of people ran with an iPod blaring into their ears. That, she thought, was cheating. Stride by stride, she built her own music. In the steady pumping of her legs and arms, she discovered each time a rhythm that was within her but also outside of her, and somehow that rhythm was one and the same. She couldn't explain it exactly, not to herself and certainly not to anyone who ever asked how she managed five miles every single day. "The rhythm of the world" – could she say that and not face laughter?

But that was it, there was no denying it. She loped into her last mile, and this was the best part. She could feel the sweat on her body, wet heat balanced against the crisp dry morning air. She felt the motion of her footsteps against the motionless ground. She felt herself upright against the pull of the earth. And in some sense that was unexplainable but undeniably true, she felt the steady drumbeat of her footfalls come into step with the trees and the lampposts and the witches' brew of human life as the world woke to a new day.

She ran. It felt good. It felt right. And at the end, approaching her apartment building at a cool-down pace, she felt both relief and regret.

Relief, because you can't run forever.

Regret, because you can't run forever.

The View

K2. One letter, one number, but to mountain climbers, it's the formula for the ultimate adventure. The world's second-highest mountain and one of the most difficult to conquer, K2 has challenged generations of climbers. Joining us now on the program is Mr. Dave English, who comes to us fresh off the journey of a lifetime: the ascent of K2. Mr. English, welcome.

Glad to be here.

You faced significant hardships on this climb, but it was nothing you haven't gone through before, I'm told?

Whenever you're twenty-eight thousand feet in the air, it's not a walk in the park, believe me. There's a lot of gear involved, all the tents and ropes and climbing equipment, plus all the food and oxygen you need to survive at that altitude. We spent a lot of time just hauling equipment around, up the next slope.

So you had people with you. This wasn't a solo expedition.

I considered that, but it didn't make sense. You don't want to take a journey without any support system. You can go farther and higher when you work together.

Who were your climbing companions, then?

I was fortunate to have two excellent Sherpa guides with me. As you know, the Sherpas are incredibly skilled in climbing and extremely knowledgeable about the terrain of K2 and throughout Pakistan and Tibet. I could not have done it without them.

There's an old joke: "Why did you climb the mountain?" And the answer is: "Because it's there." Is that why you climbed K2?

I suppose that would be one way to put it. But really it was more of a spiritual quest for me.

How so?

Well, if you really need to know, I wanted to find God. I climbed the mountain because I wanted to get close to God.

And what made you think that this was the way to God?

Well, it stands to reason, doesn't it? God's in his heaven, all's right with the world. And if the closest we can get to heaven is twenty-eight thousand feet off the ground, it seemed to me that climbing K2 would bring me that much closer to where God is.

Did you consult with any religious authorities about this plan?

No, I haven't been inside a church in a long time. Too many phonies, too much talk talk talk. And I knew I wasn't going to find God in any fancy church. I've been outdoors all my life. I figure, God made the earth, he's got to be out there somewhere.

So tell us more about the climb itself.

It was sixteen days all told, from the time we left the base camp to the time we were back. Nine days up, seven days back. Gravity helps, you know?

For the first few days it was pretty easy going. We made near ten miles the first day. But that wasn't so steep, and we had a good night's sleep and a stomach full of good food. After that it got harder and harder. We were climbing on ice, not rock. In some places it was nearly straight up, and we had to angle our way up the mountain along cracks in the ice.

The sixth day we were socked in until past noon by a terrible blizzard. I mean the snow was horizontal and the wind was fierce. I remember holding on to the supports of the tent, hoping it wasn't going to blow into the gorge below and take me with it. We didn't get far that day.

Were there points when you wanted to turn back?

Sure. Any mountain climber is lying if he tells you he never has second thoughts. There's always a point on the climb when you think to yourself, Why am I doing this? Am I nuts? I could be in a warm bed with a hot woman and a cold beer. And yet …

Yes?

There's something about the climb itself that's energizing somehow. You're exhausted and exhilarated at the same time. It might have something to do with being low on oxygen, or maybe it's just that the clear air sharpens your senses somehow. But I've never felt more alive than when I was at the edge of death on K2.

And then came the moment when you finally crested the summit.

It was afternoon, the ninth day. The guides had stayed behind a hundred yards, because they knew it was my first time. And we had spent some time talking at night, and I told them about the God thing. They're Buddhists, very spiritual people. But this idea of God didn't register with them. They think more in terms of the unity of all things – people and animals and plants and earth. "You want to see God?" one of them said to me, and he put a small rock in my hand. "You see God. Close your eyes, you see God. Open your eyes, you see God. And even when you don't, God sees you."

Anyway, they wanted to let me reach the summit first. Like I said, it almost killed me, but there's this burst of energy that carries you over the top. I stood up there and roared like a bear, like the king of the world. And there I was: twenty-eight thousand feet closer to God.

And then?

And then … nothing. I was quiet and I listened for God's voice. I was closer, so you figure I could hear it better, right? But I didn't hear anything, only the wind. I didn't hear anything, so I thought maybe I could see some sign of God, and I looked straight up, because God's in his heaven, right? And we were so high up that we were above the clouds, and it was blue and bright and clear, but I didn't see anything. Nothing. Even halfway to heaven, no sign of the big guy.

That must have been disappointing.

Sure. But only for a minute. Because on the way down, I saw God.

I beg your pardon?

You heard me.

Tell us about this experience, won't you?

We were two days into the trip down, and I was hurting. It was exhilarating making the summit, but the trip back is always a drag. You've seen it all already, right?

But this time it was different. Like I said, we were two days in, and we were coming out of the cloud layer. The clouds there are different, I swear, different from anything you can see here. They're more solid somehow. I mean, you can walk through them, but they have really defined edges. One minute you're inside the cloud, the next minute you're not.

We were climbing down a little ledge, making the next plateau, and I was halfway down when something made me turn around and look. I was plastered up against the ice, spread-eagled against the mountain, but I had to turn around. I think it must have been that we had reached the edge of the cloud, had come out the bottom of it. We were back in the land of the living.

And when I turned, I almost lost my grip right there.

What was it? What did you see?

I'm not enough of a poet to do it justice. But it was just this landscape of rock and ice and starting to be a little vegetation, a few trees, and somehow it was so sharp and perfect all of a sudden that it hit me like a slap in the face. They call that area the roof of the world, you know. It was like I was sitting on the roof looking down at my neighborhood and seeing everything I knew already but seeing it in an entirely new way.

And I got to thinking, this must be how God sees his world and all of us. I mean, we see people and trees and dogs and stuff, but God sees them from the inside out. Who invented DNA, anyway? God has to have this amazing vision of all of creation, the way if you build a bookcase or something you know every nail and every board that went into it and remember all the work that it took. And you kind of love that bookcase the way you never could love something you bought at the furniture store.

And so there I was on the roof of the world, and it seemed to me that I was seeing it through God's eyes. And I don't know, we were way below the summit by then, but I've never felt closer to God. Somehow it seemed like I was part of the whole order, and everything was exactly where it should be. And there on that ledge, God let me see it.

Mr. English, if what you've said is true, then it's only incredibly strong people like yourself, people who aren't afraid to risk dying on a mountain, it's only those people who can see God.

You don't get it, do you? God revealed himself that day. To me, sure. On a mountain. But I didn't need to make the climb, or at least I didn't need to reach the summit. God is there whether we can get it through our heads or not. But I got lucky. I got to look through God's eyes. And it seems to me that if God let a guy like me in on the secret, he's not about to hide it from everybody else.

So it's not about the mountain at all?

It's about the view from the mountain. It's about seeing the world through God's eyes. The view is all around us. You only have to look.

In the Doorway

M a t t h e w   2 5 : 3 7 - 4 0

I was working the West Side day watch, and it was early. Now that we're in one-officer patrol cars, there's no backup sitting next to you, so day watch is best. Not too many muggers and crazies out at 6 in the morning. The worst you might see is a wreck, some coffeed-up jerk plowing into something, on the road to the office way too early.

It was quiet. Which is why I stopped in the first place. Normally I would drive right by a homeless guy in Army fatigues and a fifty-day beard, huddled up in the doorway of a coin laundry before business hours. They don't bother me, I don't bother them.

But I was in a sour mood – another fight with Sheila last night on the way out the door – and I was just bored enough to want some human contact. Even if it was this no-account guy and his garbage bag full of pop cans.

"You can't stay here," I was saying as I walked up to him. The street and sidewalk were empty. I could see traffic passing on the cross street, people with places to go and things to do. "You're going to have to move along."

The man moved in stages – opened his eyes, lifted his head, sat up a little bit. He smelled like the streets – grit, alcohol and resignation. He looked me in the eye but said nothing.

"Move along. Can you? I mean, can you move?"

The man nodded slowly, as if he were thinking it over. But he didn't get up. Instead, he stretched a hand toward the doorway, inviting me to sit down.

"Wait a minute." I went back to the car and radioed 10-7. Off-duty. Then I got two Styrofoam cups and the big thermos of coffee that Sheila had poured just before she and I went sour again. That had been happening a lot lately. Seven years of marriage and you think you've got it figured out. But you never do. At least I never have.

I sat down in the doorway and poured coffee for two. God knows why. The homeless, they're not my usual drinking companions. But it was early, and it was cold, and I was ready for coffee and this guy surely was ready for his.

"Tough place to spend the night."

"I've been in worse," he said. "Spent four days once hiding out over by the landfill, when the cops were after me." His eyes rose to my badge, and he gave a half-smile. "Don't worry, I was innocent."

"Don't sweat it." I sipped the coffee, strong and black. "I've been there."

Not to the landfill – to the other side of the law. It probably was a miracle that I ended up in a patrol car instead of a prison cell. The stuff I did as a teenager – how I got away with it, I'll never know. That probably was what got me into police work. I could think like a petty crook.

We sat for a while in silence, watching the streetlights flicker out, hearing the city start to come to life. When I was just about to pack it in, figured my good deed was done for the day, he threw me a curveball. "You seem sad," he said.

Cops don't get sad, at least in public. It's part of the persona – cool, confident, on an even keel. It keeps you alive.

But I hadn't been on an even keel for maybe a year. The way it can go bad with someone, someone it's been so good with, that astonishes me. Damned right I was sad. I was also angry, and confused, and desperate to figure out where we had gone wrong. A year of this.

"Tell me," he said.

And I did. Crazy, but I told him everything – the accusations, groundless for sure but rooted in venom; the long silences that were harder than any words; the frightening feeling of disconnection where before, for once in my life, there had been someone to make me feel like I wasn't adrift in the world. I told it all, and by the end I was crying tears that were part anguish and part relief over finally having someone to say all this to. I hadn't cried since the fourth grade, when I lost a fight. The last one I ever lost, by the way.

"I understand," he said, and helped himself to more coffee. And maybe he did and maybe he didn't, but he started to talk, and it felt good to listen.

He was a veteran; I should have figured, with the fatigues. Had been through hell in some war I didn't want to ask the name of, because when he talked about war it almost strangled him.

And then, in the midst of it, he had become a pacifist. He said this without the slightest hint of irony. They say there are no atheists in foxholes, and I would have thought there were no pacifists, either. You're lobbing grenades into the jungle, you've got to get with the program, don't you?

But it turns out the Army has a bureaucracy for that just like it does for everything else. You decide you're a conscientious objector? Fine. Prove it before a panel of your peers, and presto! You're back stateside pushing paper until your four years are over.

Only it didn't work out so well. Sure, he was back in the U.S. of A., but the war was a good one and people were flying those yellow ribbons everywhere. A soldier turned peacenik – well, that was about the lowest form of coward.

So when he got out of the Army, he couldn't find work. He was a decent carpenter, but all the work was down South. Didn't have the money for school. Didn't have the desire for a car. Just wanted to watch and learn, and maybe share a little of what he had learned with whoever would listen.

Which wasn't much of anyone. So here he was: a doorway for his living room, the city mission for his meals, maybe an odd job here or there to keep body and soul together. And once in a while, a cop with a story to tell and hot coffee to tell it over.

I knew Dispatch would be sore at me for taking all this time away, so I started to make my excuses. He didn't flinch. A man used to being left behind.

But as I screwed the top back on the thermos, something made me pause.

"What you've learned," I said. "The lessons you wanted to share. What would you teach, if you had students?"

"There's only one lesson," he began, looking at me evenly. "All your universities and your books and your think tanks are fine things, but there's only one lesson. The rest is commentary."

A pause for effect. "The Beatles had it almost right," he said. "All you need is love, that's what they sang. Poor John Lennon. Look where it got him.

"But that's about *finding* love," he went on. "The lesson is this: Be about *doing* love. Sometimes love will find you, sometimes you'll find it. That's a great thing when it happens. But you can't count on it, and even when it comes, you can't count on it lasting.

"But *doing* love, that never runs out. Love is a two-way street, and when you start down that street, it always leads you to the person you need to find. Always. And sometimes that person is you."

Later, as I finished my shift and headed for home, his words came back to me. You can't count on love lasting, he had said. I thought of Sheila and the way it was slipping away with her. But *doing* love, he had said, that lasts. That's ours to own.

I thought about this, and thought about it some more. And by the time I got home, I was partway down that two-way street. Ready to do what it took. Ready to give as well as get. And ready, from the privileged seat of a police cruiser, to see evidence of that love where I could find it. Ready, after all this time, to learn the lesson.

Heart and Soul

1   C o r i n t h i a n s   1 5 : 1 2 - 2 2

PATRICIA

They say that when you're dying, in those last hours and minutes, it doesn't hurt. How it was for Johnny, I don't know. Because, of course, it happened fast. One minute he was full of life, doing things, driving – it was what he did, drive; the life of a salesman – and the next minute he was empty of life, the victim of bad timing and speed and rain and probably not paying enough attention to the road. Stupid, really. Stupid and careless, and now where I had a husband I have church ladies with their casseroles and a bed suddenly twice as big as we need. As *I* need.

They say it doesn't hurt when you're dying, and you know what? There must be something like that for the living, too, for those of us who have had a policeman ring the doorbell and tell you to sit down. Because it *doesn't* hurt. Mostly it's just *weird* – almost everything is the same, and yet you know it's going to be different from here on out. And still it doesn't hurt. How can I describe it? Like this: That time I stood up at our niece's wedding reception and the tablecloth got caught on my button, and the whole thing went crash, and it seemed the world stopped and everyone was looking at me hard. That hot-in-the-head, woozy feeling. I didn't like it. I couldn't think straight.

And so at the hospital when they asked about his organs, about turning him inside out and taking the good parts for people who need them, living people, it was easy to say yes. How often do you think about what's inside a person, anyway? I went home and my sisters came over and we tried to think of what to say to each other, and all the while the doctors were taking his corneas and his kidneys and bone tissue and some skin for burn victims.

And his heart. Especially his heart. In the movies that's how you know death has really come, when the doctor listens to his stethoscope and frowns and shakes his head. But they said Johnny's heart could live on, that there would be someone who could use it. Of course I said yes.

Funny, though. He was kind of a romantic. He always said his heart belonged to me.

KATHLEEN

For a long time, he hurt all day, every day. That can happen when the heart goes bad – your whole body is starving for blood. I used to cry, watching him try to go upstairs or even get up from a chair. But I made sure I did my crying behind closed doors. Sam was hurting, I was hurting – I didn't want it to multiply. Thirty-five years old and he moved like an old man. Luck of the draw, I guess: He was born with a heart that got weaker with every passing year.

When they put him on the list for a transplant, I almost lost it. It seemed so drastic, you know? But heart transplants happen all the time now. They gave us a pager and told us to keep our bags packed for the hospital. It took months, but finally the pager beeped. It was 5 in the afternoon. I left dinner on the stove. I didn't get home for three days.

It's funny, the things you remember. They brought the heart in a picnic cooler, straight off the helicopter. Sam was already in the O.R.; we had said our goodbyes. I cried then, couldn't help myself, and he winked at me. So brave. I remember how gaudy the colors in the waiting room were, and the TV that wouldn't turn off. I remember how tired the doctor looked when he finally came out to say it was over.

I remember what he said: "Now comes the hard part."

PATRICIA

God, it hurts. Six months since Johnny drove himself into oblivion, and missing him is what I do all day. Oh, I go to work and come home and cook dinner and once in a while I'll go to the movies, but it's like there's a hole in the universe right in front of me wherever I go. A hole shaped like Johnny.

Putting up with the well-wishers, that's another thing. I shouldn't complain. They're better than the people who cross the street when they see me coming, because they don't know what to say. But the ones who pump my hand and ask, "How are you?" with that phony kind of snap-out-of-it cheerfulness – well, what am I going to say? The truth – that I've been sucker-punched and I can't get my wind back?

But the insurance papers have cleared, and finally one day I dumped the sympathy cards into the recycling. My counselor keeps telling me it takes time, I should just wait it out, nobody rises from the ashes overnight. And so I keep going, walking around the Johnny-shaped hole in my days.

And wondering about the parts of him that live on. The corneas, the kidneys. And most especially, Johnny's heart. Does it beat on in someone's chest? Is there new life where the old one had left off?

In all of this loss, where is the hope?

KATHLEEN

He takes sixteen pills a day, and that's not going to change, but you know what? It's nothing.

Because, a year into this horrible adventure, he's back. The Sam I married, who throws a Frisbee with the kids and dances me around the kitchen and smiles when he's working in his garden, he's been given back to me.

A gift of grace. A gift of health. And maybe above all, a gift of time – time to see his daughter at her senior prom, to coach his son through a job interview. Time for us to sit on the patio together and watch the sun slipping away, not saying anything. Time for thinking. Time for sharing. A gift.

We wanted to say thank you. But the donor, he's gone, of course. The hospital doesn't tell you the details at first, only that he was a man about Sam's age and that he had died in a car accident. They make you wait a year before they'll let you try to get in touch with the family. Too emotional at first, they said. And I laughed. As if it would ever *not* be emotional, to shake somebody's hand whose loss had become your gain. Whose grief was the soil in which your hope took flower.

We talked about it, Sam and I. He wasn't sure about meeting the family. What if they didn't like us? What if they resented us, because we had something they didn't? What if they regretted the decision to donate?

But I grew up writing thank-you notes, and now I insisted. It seemed like the right thing to do. And to tell the truth, I was curious. When you adopt a child, aren't you always curious about the people who gave that baby life? Whose loss brought you joy?

And so we arranged a meeting. There was only the donor's wife. Her name was Patricia. She had been a year without her husband. We had been a year with his heart in Sam's chest.

Could we bear this encounter? Could she?

PATRICIA

They make you meet in a public place, because really, you're strangers to each other, aren't you? We did it at a restaurant, but at least we had a quiet place in the back. A semi-private room, as they say at the hospital.

Sam and Kathleen got there first. They had described themselves on the phone – tall, dark hair, a couple of kids in tow. But you know what? I think if I had been in the same baseball stadium with them, I would have known. We shared something, and I felt that bond as soon as I walked through the door.

I had expected it to be awkward. But the kids were running around, and there was bread on the table, and I don't know why, but it felt *right* somehow. Sam held out his hand, but I ignored it. I took them both in my arms and held them for a long time. What the kids thought, this strange woman bawling her eyes out and hugging her parents and they were crying too – what the kids thought, I don't know.

But here's what I knew: Life was in that room.

We get a little piece of eternity on this earth, and some of us get a bigger piece than others. Johnny's heart bought Sam and Kathleen what you couldn't buy with a million dollars: time they were in danger of losing. Like the time I lost with my husband. It never comes back. Out of loss, out of death, had come new life. At some level, I knew that. But seeing them, feeling their warm bodies full of the promise of the coming years, that brought me full circle.

"Patricia," Sam said. His voice was strong. "Would you like to hear our heart?"

And as his wife held his hand, I nestled into him like a lover, and pressed my ear into his chest, and listened hard: to the echo of a sacrifice, the miracle of the body, and the magic of a promise without end.

Remembrance Day

1 Chronicles 16:8-13

Mark 8:11-21

"Who are you again?"

Jill fought back a sigh, something that came easily when she was with her grandmother these days. "It's Jill, Grandma," she said. "I'm glad to see you."

Something flickered in the old woman's eyes, the remnant of long familiarity. "Hello, Butterfly," she said, the pet name she had given her only granddaughter when Jill was three and floating through life like a leaf on the breeze. Jill felt again the rush of pleasure she had always shared with this woman, mother of her own mother; the bond of acceptance between grown-up and child that always skips a generation. It had been a long time since she had floated anywhere. These days it seemed more like wading through mud – the kind of mud that hurricanes leave behind.

"Grandma," she said, "did you ever want something so badly that it seemed like you jinxed it – like the wanting itself made it impossible?"

She spoke almost to herself. Here in the wing of the home they called "memory care" – that was a laugh – everyone was losing whatever sharpness they ever had, like computers blowing a circuit one by one, on down the line. Freezing in slow motion. Her grandmother was no different. Jill knew that. But it felt good to talk without being challenged, to be given the space to speak truth into existence.

But the old woman surprised her. "It's that man, isn't it? You've come apart?"

"Yes. Come apart. And it feels like maybe I wanted it too much, wanted it to happen. Wanted him and me to happen."

"You're talking nonsense," her grandmother said. "Or magic. Neither one will do you any good."

"I'm hurting, Grandma. Maybe it will never happen for me."

"Maybe it won't. But maybe it will. Probably it will, if you slow yourself down."

Jill pondered that. She hadn't slowed down since before grad school. She wasn't sure she still knew how.

"Grandma," she said, "how was it for you, before Grandpa? Were there others? What was it like for you before you were married?"

Long pause. Her grandmother concentrated, her lips pursed, as if trying to find her way back from somewhere far away, trying to read the map. A furrowed hand stroked her temple.

"Butterfly," she said, "it must have been hard. But I don't remember a minute of it."

• • •

Back at work, at the lab, Jill mixed chemicals and drew samples into gleaming glass pipettes. She had learned to do the job with about half of her attention, leaving the rest free to wrestle with her problems. She went home exhausted every day.

The research was about dementia; the slogan there at PharmQuest was "Remembering the Future," holding out a dropper full of hope for those whose minds were failing. But progress had been slow. They had identified a compound that worked in mice, but backwards – it suppressed memories instead of preserving them. They had named it Forgetimax, just fooling around, Jill and the biochemical boys. The new study was testing to see if small doses of it would improve memory, the way a stimulant like Ritalin could calm down hyperactive kids.

It was easy to synthesize. There was a vial of it on the top shelf, enough for ten thousand mice. They kept the opiates under lock and key, but the experimental stuff they didn't bother to lock up. No one would want it, was the theory.

Her workday over, Jill washed up in the gleaming steel sink. She hung up her white lab coat and that awful hairnet, and put on her jacket. Nowhere to go tonight. Nothing left of the life she had been hoping for, the specific new reality she had imagined, a life with the give-and-take of two human beings shoring each other up along the way.

Her grandmother had lived long; it seemed a cruelty that in her last years she would be denied her memories. Ha, thought Jill. What I wouldn't give for some of that forgetfulness right about now. All the pain of the breakup, all the sick sadness of hope denied – just leave it all behind. Wash the synapses clean.

She reached for the light switch, and her eyes went toward the shelf. Amber liquid in a clear glass vial. Forgetimax.

Insane, she thought. The stuff had never been tested in humans. There was no way of knowing the effective dose, or the lethal one for that matter. There was no telling how it would work, or if it would. All she knew was that she couldn't bear the tape running in her head, the latest chapter in a painful story.

She was alone in the lab. She picked up the vial, swished the liquid around. She was beyond the point of caution.

"What does not kill me makes me stronger," she said out loud, and poured 50 cc's into a test tube, and drank it down fast, before she could change her mind.

• • •

It didn't kill her. That was the first thing she thought of, the next morning, after an excellent sleep. She remembered the drink, could still taste the acetone in it. She remembered the drive home and the evening, remembered the 11 o'clock news. But everything before that night, it was as if wet cotton had covered it over. Only the vaguest sense remained of her life before. She could recall names, but not the stories behind them; faces, but not the love or curiosity or attraction they sometimes inspired.

A cast-off T-shirt in her dresser drawer drew her up short. It was his, she knew, but she didn't know what to make of it. She put it to her face and breathed in, monitoring her body for the familiar rapid heartbeat and adrenaline rush, the chemical dance of mating. Nothing. If you asked her, she could tell you the man's name but not the color of his eyes or the timber of his laugh or the way he touched her hair. She remembered facts; she remembered nothing.

There was no pain.

Jill dressed and went for her Saturday ritual: coffee and a Boston cream doughnut. The shop on the corner had the best. She had discovered it not long after she had moved to this strange city; ever since it had been an oasis, the sweet caffeinated echo of times when she felt rescued from her lostness.

Tina the owner served them up without asking. Jill sat in the window and drank and ate. She could feel the coffee warming her, loosening her limbs and her insides, calling her brain to attention. The sugar overpowered her taste buds, as it always did. Good, good … but where had these tastes lived in her, before yesterday? The shop was the same, the waitress, the food; but something was missing deep within. Somewhere inside her was the memory of a hundred Saturdays in this Formica booth. That she knew. But the wet cotton was intact. She left still hungry for something.

And yet, there was no pain.

The next day she went to the park and joined her friend Theresa for a run. They had met the first time at the park, almost bumped into each other, and discovered that they had the same style of running: slow and long. The goal was to keep moving, keep talking and work the tension out of their backs and legs.

She didn't tell Theresa about the Forgetimax. A little experiment, to keep it private. Mile piled upon mile, and soon enough they were ready to quit.

At least Theresa was.

"More?" she gasped, as Jill nodded her head toward the road. "I'm tapped out. You're not feeling it?"

Jill listened to her body. Shoulders, limp. Back, calm. Legs, relaxed.

Just as they were at the beginning.

"OK," she said, her voice strangely distant. The run had tired her out, but she was missing the thrill of rediscovering her muscles, reclaiming them from the fists of tension by which her body held onto its past. The sweet release of exertion had been denied her.

No pain. But strangely, not so much pleasure, either. The sweetness seemed to have drained out of her days like sap from a spring maple. Without the memory of loss and sorrow as well as joy and triumph, she teetered on a foundation that was built partly out of shadows. Beneath her feet was the uncertainty of missing a piece of her life, of not knowing who she was. There was just nowhere to stand.

◆ ◆ ◆

Sunday afternoons, they served a special dinner at the home. It made a good time to visit. This was one of her grandmother's good days, and as Jill spread the napkin on her lap and opened a split of Chianti, they had the gift of a conversation.

"You're crazy, Butterfly," her grandmother said with affection. "Putting chemicals into your brain like that. It could have killed you."

Jill, chastened, said nothing.

"And for what? To live as if you've never lived? To put a smiley face over reality?"

Jill poured the wine. She gave her grandmother a piece of bread, good crusty Italian, and cut one for herself. She broke them and brought a piece to her lips. Her grandmother did the same.

They ate, and Jill remembered.

Remembered the times they had cooked and then eaten together, just the two of them. Remembered the richness of her grandmother's life, set off now by the dissipation of her decline. And remembered, suddenly, with a flood of gratitude, her own difficult and frustrating and surprising life, incomplete like everyone's, but made fuller by the way tough and tender wound like grapevines around her wounded heart. Her grateful heart. Her heart full of a grace that, she now realized, never let her suffer alone.

"Grandma," she said, raising her glass, "thanks for the memories. Drink deep. To life."

On the Balcony

I s a i a h   5 8 : 1 1

SPRING

Something skitters across the sidewalk, and the boy pulls up short. Not that he's going anywhere particular. At seven years old he's on nobody's schedule. At seven years old you're beneath the radar screen for most people.

"Sorry!" A voice from above.

He looks up.

"Could you bring that back up here? They're kind of expensive, and I need every one."

The boy finds the thing that has stopped him – a brown lump of something vegetable. He hesitates, looks around him. He has never been into this particular apartment building, and his mother has warned him against strangers. But the old woman looks harmless. He jumps and gets a hand on the bottom reaches of the fire escape, then walks up the four stories to her balcony. He digs into his pocket and pulls out the mystery thing.

"Thank you." The old woman smiles at him. "Dutch tulip bulbs. A dollar apiece. I can't afford to be losing any."

She looks familiar, but he can't quite place her. It's like he's known her a long time, but he's never really known her.

He asks her name. The old woman smiles again, silent, and goes back to her digging. She's planting four window boxes, but they're not much to look at. Just clumpy dirt with sticks and stuff all through it, and rocks. It doesn't look like dirt you could grow anything in.

The boy asks her name again.

"I'm here, and you're here. It's enough," she says, mysteriously. Digging. Turning over the hard bad soil, trying to get some air and space and hope into it. "How about giving me a hand?"

She hands him a little shovel like he's never seen before and tells him to mix in some stuff that looks like sawdust. He is seven years old and he does what he's told. They work side by side in the late-morning sun, not saying much. The boy asks no more questions, just watches and does what she does. He picks rocks and sticks out of the soil and crumbles it between his fingers. It smells like the city is far away.

Morning turns to afternoon. The boxes fill up.

The old woman brings out a shiny aluminum gizmo, a sharp bright cone with a handle on top. She pushes it into the soil and pulls it out again, leaving a neat little hole. The boy gives her a bulb from a burlap sack of them, and she nestles it into place and shows him how to fill around it so that just the tip of the bulb peeks from the ground. They go on that way, scooping, planting, filling in, until the burlap sack is empty.

"Go," she says. "You've done well. This building needs some color, and now there will be flowers."

He turns back, a question on his lips.

"When?"

But the old woman is already half through the door to the apartment, gesturing him away, with a look in her eyes. *Don't ask,* it says. *Trust.*

SUMMER

It's almost as if his body is newly minted and he is discovering what it can do. The boy is running, not from anyone or toward anything, but running because the amazingness of his legs and arms impels him forward. The city air is thick and hot, but the boy is strong at fifteen and he breathes easily.

As he rounds the corner he looks upward, and sure enough the window boxes are out again this year. He looks around for police, then reaches up to the familiar fire escape and climbs to the old woman's balcony. He knocks and she comes to the door.

"I'm glad you're here," the old woman says. "See this? It's called a trellis. I want you to help me put it in place. I've got some vines this year, and they need a place to spread out."

The boy does as he's told, but he's impatient. It seems to take forever. And what's the point? The plants in the window boxes are just beginning to come into leaf, little fingers of delicate green setting off the rich soil. They're late. By this time of the season, they should be blossoming like the girls at the city swimming pool. The old woman is an optimist, that's for sure, but even he can tell that it's a lean year for her garden.

The trellis in place, she sends the boy on his way. He decides to jump from the bottom of the fire escape, and he hits the ground running. He wonders about her silence. He keeps his questions close to the heart.

AUTUMN

He has a name, and it's Daddy. "Daddy, take us with you." "Daddy, when are you coming home?" "Daddy, what did you bring me?"

And he loves it, loves the whole Daddy thing, but it came on with such swiftness that he looks back and can barely remember how he got to this place, a place defined by a family and a job and the endless mortal combat of buying and bills. There isn't time for a garden. There's barely time to brush his teeth in the morning.

The boy is a Daddy and all his gains are neck-and-neck with what he's lost.

But this day he takes the kids driving and decides to check out the old neighborhood, and he has told them so much about the old woman and her window boxes that they demand to see, and it has been years but he pulls up to the apartment building and darned if she isn't out there pruning this year's flowerbeds. An explosion of flowers. A good year.

They take the stairs, the boy and his kids. Parenthood makes one cautious.

It's astonishing how little the old woman has changed. There are introductions all around, and the kids know better than to ask her name, because they've heard the story of the first time he met her, just like they've heard the love story of their parents before they became parents and were just people. They go out onto the balcony and look at the flowers.

"I decided to switch to peonies," the old woman says. "The tulips never did so well up here. And mums, I did mums – you can't kill them even if you try."

The colors are so bright, they almost hurt his eyes. The kids fuss with the flowers and the old woman doesn't object. She deadheads a few and shows them how, and they curl up next to the window boxes and pick away, grooming them, absorbed as he has seen them with crayons and paper. Making beauty, or discovering it.

The boy who is a Daddy sits for a spell and drinks it in, the old woman, the all-consuming kids he loves, this splash of growing things in the middle of a dead brick building. The old woman catches his eye and winks, something she has never done before in his presence. It's as if they share a secret knowledge. She pins a flower to each child's shirt, and the boy who is a Daddy gets one too. It smells like his little girl's hair.

WINTER

The boy is walking again, but it's not easy. Arthritis, and the slow parade of indignities that march in as the decades pass. The cane helps.

With the kids grown and gone, the boy who is an old man spends a lot of time listening now. It gets easier in winter, when snow muffles the car tires and keeps the neighbors inside. The boy listens – for what, he doesn't exactly know – listens as he walks the city streets, home again. Circle of life, he thinks, except that circles have no end and life looks shorter every time he lets himself think about it.

The boy listens, and he hears humanity in all its messy complexity. He hears lovers and music and laughter; he hears babies crying and mourners weeping; he hears the hot breath of the runners and the inhuman beeping of hospital machines. Some days it makes sense, some days it makes him wince, as if no good could ever come of it.

He walks. He listens. He wonders.

And then, this day, he turns down the street where the old woman lives, knowing she can't possibly still be there. Our ground time here will be brief. The snow crunches under his feet.

The apartment house stands where it always has. Not much has changed.

The boy looks upward, and his ragged progress down the sidewalk stops short. In the window is the old woman, astonishingly unchanged, watching out the window with a look that is half lover's gaze and half musician's concentration. Watching as the winter closes in.

On the balcony, in the dead of winter, the window boxes are in full bloom. And as the boy looks, he is stunned to discover boxes overflowing with flowers at every window – peonies and mums, tulips and daffodils, daisies, petunias, pansies, phlox, black-eyed Susans. The boy feels dizzy in the cold air. Reds and yellows and violets shock his eyes against the white of the snow.

The boy reaches up and taps the fire escape with his cane, for old times' sake. He does not know whether the old woman has seen him. He thinks she probably has. He thinks she doesn't miss much.

He walks. He listens. And as he heads home, to his warm house with the floral wallpaper, snowflakes fall on a building in bloom, and the old woman watches, and it looks like an early spring.

Soldier's Home

L u k e   2 4 : 1 - 1 2

The soldier is home, and he has a son.

The son has spent the time thinking about his father at war, and even though they've explained to him that it's not like the wars he has seen starring John Wayne, all horses and white hats and one-bullet victories, he imagines his father as the hero in a story where only the heroes have faces. He cannot know that for his father danger comes with faces a lot like his own, the young, the easily misled. The son has not worried much, for he knows that his father is strong and has a smile that can set the world right.

Now the soldier is home.

And the boy, though he doesn't have the words to say it, can feel the difference. The cigarettes, for instance; where before the soldier smoked them outside, and only a few, carefully shielding his family from the perils of breathing, now he sits in the living room and the ashtray is mounded beside him. The smoke is a hazy picture frame around the soldier, and the son sees that the picture has changed. Something in his father has died, and in the space left behind has grown a place where the soldier thinks deeply and knows more than he wants to say.

The son has written for his teacher a composition. It is a list of ways his father is a hero. The soldier finds it in the kitchen one afternoon when all is quiet, and he reads the list, and he goes to the boy's bedroom and takes the plastic rifle, an uncle's gift, and the soldier, gently, quietly, walks out to the garage and throws it in the trash.

◆ ◆ ◆

The soldier is home, and he has a wife.

And she has been warned that it will be different, afterward. The Army has learned some things as it gets better at war. One thing it has learned is that families suffer. And so she has gone to gatherings where this man she loves, whom she has loved since they were in the tenth grade, is classified and analyzed as if he were somehow like all the others. "Your soldier," they kept calling him, in the gatherings. As in: "Your soldier faces a difficult adjustment to civilian life."

The wife knows this, knows that of course the life she shares with him is different from a life of patrols and explosives, suspicion and boredom, a life of sleeping on cots and practicing black humor with his blood brothers. Two months in, she knows that her soldier needs time. Still, she can't help it when resentment colors her daily round with the job, the house, the kids. This is the life, *their* life, that she held together, plugging holes in a leaky ship, while he was a world away. "Don't expect your soldier to fall immediately back into the old routines," said the Army counselor. And bitterly she sees the truth in that. The soldier is home, a home that has lain like a fallow field waiting for the plow, and some piece of him won't cooperate in reclaiming the way it used to be.

It's a delicate calculus, making a home, sharing a home. He has reclaimed the checkbook and the TV remote, and she knows that the soldier is not the only one who has changed. To hold a family together is no small accomplishment. Now the soldier is home, and he is changed, but she is changed as well. She wonders, late at night, who will make the pieces fit back together.

She stays carefully to her side of the bed, so as not to startle his sleep. When he reaches for her, his hand feels rougher than she remembered.

• • •

The soldier is home, and he has a daughter.

And she knows, because she has seen her friends with their fathers, that something happens between teenage girls and their fathers. She loved him as a child, of course, but saw him almost as a force of nature, as if he had always been there, as immovable as the thick maple in the back yard. Now – and it's not because he went away to war; she knows this because her friends too have changed, friends whose fathers have stayed – now she has come to the astonishing realization that the soldier could be a person who worries, and sleeps late sometimes, and likes mango but not papaya, who listens to strange music when he's driving alone.

She sees the way he looks at her mother, and she has come to realize that there are things between men and women that she does not yet know. She feels herself on the edge of something that may be a hill or may be a precipice. And she looks at the soldier, who is home now and does not notice her watching, and she sees a man and imagines for a moment that he is her man, and what that would mean, what men do, what women do; what husbands and wives do to make the world work, to invent a world between them.

And then one day she comes home from swim practice and the dog gets out and there is the scratch of brakes and the dog's piteous yelp. The soldier brushes past her on the doorstep at a dead run. She watches him in the street, a few words with the driver, not angry, and he comes back with the dog in his arms. They take her to the vet and nothing is broken, and they come home and the soldier holds the dog on his lap on the couch, stroking her head hypnotically, the crisis over, and the daughter is surprised that she isn't surprised to see that his face is glistening with tears.

• • •

The soldier is home, and he has a father.

And the father, too, was a soldier, back in the last good war. He has not talked about it much, even to his son. There are some things that cannot be spoken, because memory can be a tyrant and he has a family to take care of. He has built a good life in a country he defended, and he is proud of it.

Now the soldier is home and still there are things that cannot be spoken, but the father knows they will find their own way into the world. He has some country property, and one Saturday he asks the soldier and the boy to come do some work.

He wants to plant some grapes, has always dreamed of being a gentleman-farmer with a wine press in the garage, and the land is good for it. But snaking through the middle of it is a tumbledown stone fence, remnant of the time when property lines were something the cattle had to respect. If he is to plow, the wall has to go.

And so on this Saturday, with the sun low in the east but already warm, they ride a tractor out into the land and begin the labor of the ancients, moving stones from one place to another. They had thought the boy would be mostly moral support, but he proves surprisingly strong. They give him the one pair of work gloves they have, and he starts from the top and heaves stones into the trailer with finesse. He is proud of his muscle; he comes from a long line of hard workers.

The soldier and his father join in, not saying much, just rhythmically hefting the stones and tossing them into the trailer. Chips and dust fly as the stones clatter onto the pile; slowly the field gets lighter and the trailer gets heavier. They tow it to the far corner, dump the load, then come back for more.

The sun is higher and hotter now. The boy is slowing down and already thinking about lunch. The soldier has not slowed down. In fact, as his father watches, the soldier attacks this wall of stones with something like anger. He bends and lifts and hauls and throws, and trots back to do it again. Sweat has plastered his hair to his forehead, and the dust of ancient rocks has smudged his face. The soldier grunts as he lifts the heaviest rocks, and he throws them hard into the trailer. Throws them with authority. Throws them to get them out of the way.

His hands, the father sees, are scraped and cut from the sharp edges of the stones. There are streaks of blood where he has wiped the sweat from his face.

The soldier attacks the wall of stones, and as he works, the father and the boy ease off and draw away, and soon they are standing together, watching. The soldier bends and lifts and hauls and throws. Anger. Relief. Release.

The wall is nearly gone. The father feels it down deep. He goes to the soldier and takes his shoulder and leads him to the side and sits him down next to his son. Then the father goes to the tractor and comes back with gauze and tape, and he takes the soldier's hands and binds them up, the right hand and then the left, and the soldier looks and the father is bleeding as well, so the soldier tapes his hands up, and the boy of course wants tape too, so he takes the gloves off and they take turns, his grandfather and his father, take turns binding up the wounds of his human work, wounds that he will come to know in time, wounds whose pain they know all too well, wounds that come when you take down a wall in the heat of the Saturday sun.

The Ties
That Unbind

Mark 10:17-31

The phone rings. I pick it up.

"Mr. Kenyon?" the voice says. "It's Marcia. The wedding planner? People are mostly here at the church, and it's getting kind of late, and I'm wondering when you'll be here. We need to get your boutonniere in place and get the processional in order. It's bad luck for a wedding to start late."

She stops talking. *That's* unusual.

"Mr. Kenyon?"

"Just getting myself together, Marcia," I say. "I'll be over in a few minutes."

I hang up, tug at the collar of this rented tuxedo. Too tight. Everything about this day – this long-anticipated, long-dreaded day – feels like it's choking me.

Julie, my little girl. A prize wrapped in white linen, to be given away to one lucky winner.

Not that I have anything against Justin. He seems like a fine young man, in the old-fashioned phrase, and he has some ambition. All these kids speak computer like a second language, and computers run the world now – he'll make his living somewhere. And he treats my daughter like a porcelain vase, something precious and rare.

Which she is, of course. Precious and rare. And exasperating.

Let Marcia wait. I can sit for a few minutes, and remember.

◆ ◆ ◆

Julie was only eight years old, and in the fourth grade. I know because her teacher was Miss Roberts, who used to be a cheerleader for the Oakland Raiders. Her parent-teacher conferences were always well-attended. Even the fathers wanted to go.

We sat at those tiny school desks, Melinda and I, my legs scrunched into the aisle, and listened as Miss Roberts talked about Julie and what her life was like in those long hours she was at school. "She's a special kid," the teacher said. "Doing great in all her subjects, a good reader, doesn't cause trouble."

Special, we said. What did she mean?

"Let me tell you what happened Tuesday," Miss Roberts said. "It was just when we were getting ready to go to lunch, so it was kind of organized chaos, the kids digging out their lunches and their money. Julie was over in the back with her friend Patrick. They were looking at the GameBoy she had brought for show-and-tell."

"Her big birthday present," Melinda said. "She loves that game."

"I know," Miss Roberts said. "She talked so long about it, I had to tell her to go sit down. Then there she was with Patrick, and they were looking at the game, and I could see her thinking for a moment. Then she just handed it over it to him."

"That little thug!" I said.

"No, it wasn't a shakedown," the teacher said. "I talked to her about it. She said she just wanted to give it to him. I told her she should talk to her parents. Did she?"

"No," my wife said. "We'll talk to her about it."

Which we did, as soon as we got home. Julie was on the phone. It starts early, this impulse in women to weave themselves together with words.

"I just wanted Patrick to have it," she said to us. "He loves GameBoy but his parents won't get him one. He can only play it at his friend's house."

"But we thought *you* liked it yourself," I said.

"Oh, I did, Daddy," she assured me. "It was a great birthday present."

I made that noise that Melinda always hated, a cross between a growl and a sigh, my standard reaction to every frustration.

"Julie," I said. "It's good to be generous. That's a fine thing. But that GameBoy was kind of expensive. And we got it for *you*. Did you really have to give it away?"

She looked at me with a level assurance that made her seem like a wise old soul. "Daddy," she said, and her tone was serious. "I liked it, but Patrick *loved* it. If I kept it, every time I played I would be thinking of him and how he wasn't playing. It needs to be in his house. Which reminds me . . ."

"Hmm?"

"Can I go to play at Patrick's tomorrow after school?"

◆ ◆ ◆

Like I said, exasperating sometimes. I tug at my collar again, rub at a scuff on these impossibly glossy black shoes. This day is costing me more than the down payment we made on our first house, that little ranch just big enough for three.

That was a long time ago. The days are long, the years are short. I have worked hard to get us to this place – a bigger house for a smaller family, now that Melinda is gone; a good retirement account, some money in the bank, cars that can be trusted to start even in the deep freeze of January. Security can be hard to come by; a lot of people live every day fearful that the bills will overwhelm the money at the end of the month. I've been lucky, I know. And yet it never seems enough.

Maybe that's because I know it can disappear. Everything can disappear, can escape your grasp.

I should get to the church. But suddenly I am overcome with the sadness that runs just below the surface of our lives, the great sadness that came like an overnight fog and still clouds every moment.

That was eight years ago. Julie was sixteen – two-thirds of the way to her wedding day. A day her mother really should be here for.

• • •

The cancer had spread quickly, and it was clear that within a few days Melinda would be gone. We were at home, thank God; the blessings of hospice care. I had settled in for the last vigil. Her mother insisted that Julie keep up her regular school schedule, though I don't know how she was able to learn anything. She cried for an hour every night when she went to bed, and I know that Melinda's heart ached for her.

Mine did too. I was going to lose Melinda; I didn't know how I could possibly live through that. And yet that's the deal you make when you love someone: Someday one of you will stand over a casket and weep. For me it was just happening sooner than it should. But Melinda's death would drive an iron stake into Julie's childhood. Would drive blackness into her sunny soul. For Melinda, for me, for Julie, the utter unfairness of the whole thing was galling.

Julie was just home from school and was by her mother's bedside, smelling of fresh air in that antiseptic sickroom. The hospice aide had just left. Julie was very still, her breathing synchronized with Melinda's, like lovers imprinting on each other. I watched from the doorway.

"Sweetheart," her mother said, "I need to tell you something."

Julie was silent, listening.

"I know how hard this is for you," Melinda began.

"For *me*?" Julie said. "I'm not the one who's ... sick."

"Dying," her mother corrected her. "Don't be afraid to say it. *I'm* not afraid."

I saw tears ease down Julie's face. Melinda reached out and took her hand.

"Julie," she said, "sometimes I think the Buddhists are right. It's our attachments that make us suffer. We need to learn how to let go."

"I can't let go," she said through her tears. "I need you here. What will we do without you?"

"You'll do fine," Melinda said crisply. "You'll take care of your father, and he'll take care of you. There will be life in this house. Thus says She Who Must Be Obeyed."

I smiled. Her old self-mocking imperious title, dragged out when she had made up her mind about something.

"Here's what I want to tell you," Melinda said. "This is hard-won wisdom, a great secret that only old people get to learn. I'm telling it to you now, and it will make sense when you need it. It's about love. Here's what I know: We think of love as something that happens between two people, like an amazing force field. But it seems to me that love is more like the ocean, and we're the fish. Do you think fish even notice the water? I think we don't even notice the love, most times. I love your father, I love you. When I'm gone, I'm gone. But there will be just as much love in your life. The world is organized to make love grow and deepen and expand. And so is the next life. I'm sure of it."

She lay back on the pillow, exhausted by the effort of speech.

"But Mom, I can't let go of you."

"You can," Melinda said. "You will. And so will I. Death is the final letting-go; you just have to trust that someone's there to catch you. Besides" – her eyes glinted, that impish look I had always loved – "like they say on the comedy club circuit, dying is easy. Comedy is hard."

I start my search for the car keys. Can't find anything these days. Melinda used to know where everything was; she knew me so well she knew where I misplaced things.

Find them. Climb carefully into the car so as not to mess up the tuxedo. Head toward the church.

♦ ♦ ♦

I took Julie to college three years after Melinda died. She had taken a map and drawn a circle sixty miles in radius, and applied to every substantial school inside it. Finally she had chosen one right on the border, an hour's drive from home. Not too far to come home, but far enough to discourage Dad from just dropping in.

I hauled the impossibly large stack of her stuff up to the room, met her roommate, hooked up the stereo and the TV. There were a bunch of young men in red shirts, the Welcome Team, milling around, and I was glad of their strong backs even as I watched them look Julie up and down, approvingly. She would not be in her own bed in my house tonight. I would just have to live with that.

But she was a good girl. I knew that.

And then we were in the parking lot. She was wearing a baseball cap in the school colors, backwards like a rapper, but of course on her it was cute and not thuggish. She was like a violet that had been transplanted into a bigger pot – it might take a few days, but she would flourish in this place.

Meanwhile, I would be sixty miles away and I knew I needed to stay there.

"Thanks, Dad," she said. "I think we've got it all."

I pulled out my wallet and gave her a hundred dollars. "Keep this someplace safe," I said. "Don't get caught short. Take care of yourself."

"Daddy," she said. "You know I love you."

"I know."

She understood me so well.

"You'll live through this," she said.

"I know."

"I'll call you." She gave me a hug, tight and quick, and then she was off, the bill of her cap waving at me as she trotted away.

In a very quiet car, I drove home alone.

♦ ♦ ♦

And now again I am alone and driving, this time toward her instead of away. Toward Julie, toward Justin. Toward Marcia the wedding planner, who I am sure will scold me for my tardiness and tut-tut over my flyaway hair. Toward a ceremony where I will give away my daughter – curious expression, that – to the man who has already replaced me at the center of her universe. As it should be.

In the church parking lot, I crick my neck to look to the top of the steeple, and squint into the sunshine. The sexton will ring the bell when the vows are complete.

I'm pretty sure that they don't see everything up there in heaven. But I wonder if Melinda will hear the bells. "We don't even notice the love, most times," she said. With empty arms and open hands, I'm going to try to notice it. The sound of bells goes on for a long, long ways.

PART 2

Reclaiming the story

The Wondrous Stranger

L u k e   2 4 : 1 3 - 3 5

My name is not important. At least that's what Luke thought. Cleopas found his way into the Gospel, but we women haunt the edges of the story, faceless and silent.

My name is not important. But no matter. My story – that is important. Because I am a witness to the risen Christ. Three days after his death, I have seen the Lord.

This is a story of the heart and the eyes. It is a story of magic, but it began in the most ordinary of ways: with a walk home.

We were on our way back home to Emmaus after the awful events of that Passover weekend. A seven-mile walk, but it seemed like seventy. Our hearts were heavy, for the man we had hoped would finally free Israel from the Romans was dead, never to return. It was agony to see centurions on the road; to our eyes, they were gloating with power.

Never since our first days together have my husband and I been so deep in discussion. We couldn't stop talking, trying to make sense of it all. When the stranger came to us on the road – and I shouldn't say this, because hospitality is everything, of course – when the stranger came, it was a bother to let him into our little world. He seemed to come out of nowhere – strange in that flat land.

We wanted to be alone with our grief and our perplexity. We needed to walk off our sorrow.

But there he was, his sandals scraping along with ours. And when he spoke, we could not ignore him.

"What's this you're discussing so intently?" he asked.

Cleopas rolled his eyes. I was embarrassed – and afraid. It was dangerous to speak of these things.

"Are you the only one in Jerusalem who hasn't heard what's happened in the last few days?" my husband said.

"What? What's happened?"

Cleopas looked at me, incredulous.

I spoke. I know I shouldn't have, in the presence of a man not my husband. But my heart was breaking, and my words were almost like tears. I had to get them out.

"Jesus the Nazorean. That's who we're talking about. You don't know him? He was a prophet, one of the great ones."

On the stranger's lips, the hint of a smile. I felt the anger rise in my face.

"But he is dead!" I cried. "The chief priests and scribes handed him over; they passed a death sentence, and they crucified him. Crucified him, like a common bandit! The one who we had hoped would redeem Israel."

"When was all this?"

"Three days ago – this is the third day, I mean. But that's not all. Some of the women in our group – Mary Magdalene, Joanna, and Mary the mother of James – they went to the tomb where this Jesus lay, to anoint him, of course. This was first thing in the morning, but when they got there, the stone had been rolled away, and the body was gone!"

"We suspect grave robbers," Cleopas put in. "But why? He had no gold or finery."

"But the angels," I said to my husband. And to the stranger: "The women told us they had seen angels there. At the tomb, I mean. And the angels said that Jesus was alive! We went to see for ourselves, some of us did, and they were right: The body was gone. But no angels. And no Jesus.

"We don't know what to think. My husband suspects a plot, but I know those women; they wouldn't make this up, about the angels. So we were trying to understand, here on the road. And then you came."

The stranger looked at us. His eyes were dark and deep; a mystery lived there.

"Consider the prophets," he said. And so he began, speaking with authority, like a teacher with the key to all knowledge.

Oh, he knew the Torah. He started with the books of Moses, and he didn't stop: Isaiah. The Psalms. The Book of Daniel. Even Micah and Habbakuk. "Let not your hearts be troubled," the stranger said. "The Messiah *had* to suffer. It is as it has been written."

We walked and listened. And a peculiar sensation came, at least for me. My heart, where all the emotions lie – it was as if my heart was burning to hear this, on fire for knowing how these days could fit into the history of our people. As we walked, as the stranger spoke, the dead weight in my chest burned clean and hot and pure, like the holy bush before Moses.

I stole a look at my husband. He could not take his eyes off the stranger. His step was light, like mine had become. We walked. We listened.

It was almost sunset when we came near to our little home. The sun was red in the west; finally the cool of evening was approaching.

We reached our turnoff. The stranger kept walking.

"Wait!"

He turned.

"Stay with us. It's almost nightfall. You can't go much farther."

The stranger seemed to consider this. "I couldn't impose."

"Stay," said Cleopas. "We insist."

My husband is not a man you can say no to. The stranger nodded, and the three of us went inside.

I hurried up the dinner. The men sat in the other room, and there was no more talk. Each seemed caught up in his own thoughts. The only sound was the bleating of the goats outside, and the fire crackling under the soup pot.

We sat to eat. "Please, sit here," my husband said, motioning the stranger to the head of the table.

You're supposed to refuse such a gesture. But the stranger took the place of honor as if he had been there all his life. My husband and I exchanged glances.

The stranger looked at the meal and looked at us. He took the loaf and bowed his head in blessing.

My heart burned within me. Holy fire.

The stranger broke the bread and gave it to us.

Hear me, listener. I am a woman of sound mind and good character. I am not much given to the weakness of imagination. And so know that what I tell you is true and can be trusted:

It was the Messiah. There at our table. As he broke the bread, we saw the cruel wounds in his hands, but we saw also the love in his eyes.

Without words, this we gave him in return. We looked in awe and trembling and a dawning sense that the impossible had come to pass.

Jesus the Christ was here.

And then, just like that, as we reached for the bread, he was gone. As quietly as he had joined us on the road, he departed; we know not how.

God be praised.

We walk now on the same road, the Emmaus road, but back the other way, to Jerusalem to tell the disciples. Or rather, we run. Or maybe it's floating, or flying like the birds.

Our hearts burn. Christ is risen. We have seen the Messiah.

And as we go, on this road and the next, we are filled to the breaking point of joy with that knowledge. An ordinary man, this wondrous stranger, was the living Christ at our side and at our table. In the breaking of the bread, we knew him.

We look at every face now, watching for signs of that love. We can't take a chance that we'll miss him.

Christ is among us. Watch for him.

As the Stone Flies

1   S a m u e l   1 7

As soon as the smooth river stone left his sling, David could see the end of the story. He had launched enough stones to feel when one was true. But as sometimes happens, its progress through the air seemed to take forever. Even the throaty roar of the opposing armies fell silent behind the beating of his heart and the rush of his blood. Time seemed to have slowed; every inch was an eternity. The stone crossed the distance between the two warriors, and as it did, David remembered …

Remembered the long days tending his father's sheep. At twenty, he had been doing that for half a lifetime. He didn't mind it, not really. It was his father's order, and when a boy has seven older brothers, he does what he can to get himself noticed. Jesse was an old man now, and David reflected that even now his father seemed to look *through* him. As if the boy were an afterthought long forgotten.

Even when he brought the flock home from a day's grazing and had tales to tell. There were lions in the scrubby, arid landscape, and bears. Sometimes they came out of nowhere and snatched up a sheep unwise enough to stray from the herd. David had learned to put his adrenaline to good use in those times, leaping for the sling and stones, challenging the predator with good aim and a boldness he didn't always feel. But it had always worked out; no bear's menacing paws had slashed his skin, and mostly he had kept the flock in safety.

As if Jesse noticed. In this family, the shadow of the brothers was long – especially the firstborn, Eliab, tall and handsome and strong. A warrior.

But David felt at home with the sheep. In the wilderness, he could play his lute and sing his songs and have long conversations with the living God, the God of Israel. His songs were simple and strong. "The Lord is my shepherd," one of them began. "I shall not want."

The stone was in the air. David remembered.

He remembered the long walk, twelve miles, from Bethlehem to the Valley of Oaks. His three eldest brothers were encamped there with the Israelite army, struggling to keep the vicious Philistine forces at bay. Wild rumors surrounded these People of the Sea. Rumors of evil. And certainly it was true that they had mastered the working of iron; their shields and their armor were far superior to the Israelites'. Only blood and bravery would keep them from the holy city of Jerusalem.

A long walk, because his father had made him take provisions to his brothers. He had set out at dawn, the sun casting long shadows before him. But the bread and cheese were beside the point, really. The two armies had been blustering at each other across the broad valley for forty days, and it was looking like the fight was coming. The old man was sick with worry. It was David's task to bring news of his brothers' welfare. For his own sake as well as theirs, he hoped his return would not be with bad news.

When he got to the camp, he could hear the whoops of young men on the brink of battle. High on excitement; high on fear. He trotted after them, found his brothers, and watched – in this gentle valley, where his sheep could have grazed and he could have heard the voice of God in the brook – David watched as two armies came so far but no farther, bristling with armor but not yet ready to throw the first spear.

It was then that he heard the challenge.

The stone was thrown so hard it whistled. David remembered.

He remembered how the massive Philistine separated from his men and walked toward them like a schoolyard bully. "Servants of Saul!" he shouted, starting with a vicious insult. They were servants of God, of course, not the king.

"Choose a man for yourselves, and send him to me. One on one. I defy you! If he can fight me and kill me, we'll be your servants. But if I prevail, then you shall serve us. Who will it be?"

He said it with the practiced air of long repetition, and David would come to know that the soldier had made this challenge morning and night for forty days. But the words were no less terrifying for their familiarity. David watched as the Israelites backed away, then turned tail and ran like frightened sheep. His brothers were among them. The warriors.

And when they had taken refuge at the camp, he tried to understand. The Philistine was huge, anyone could see that, fearsome in his armor and his anger. But the power of the living God – well, that was on the Israelites' side of the valley. He was perplexed that these soldiers of Yahweh wouldn't know that power. What did they have to fear?

He asked some more questions. He was still asking when Eliab his brother approached with a sneer. "Isn't it time you ran along?" said the older one. "Go back to your lousy sheep. I know you – you're a tourist here. Well, it isn't a show."

"What have I done now? It was only a question," David replied sullenly. All his past humiliations at Eliab's hand came flooding back. He felt his face reddening to match his hair. He turned away.

The stone flew straight and true. The Philistine was looking right at him, the great forehead exposed. And David remembered.

He remembered being summoned before the king, because his words had spread through the camp. Saul had made some mistakes; everyone knew that, including the king himself. And so Saul was tentative, unsure of himself. Searching for answers.

The Philistine had promised single combat. Man against man; the loser's army would be vanquished. It was a cleaner way to fight, but more than that, it was a clear demonstration of the power of righteousness. Because in single combat, one's god fought alongside. As much as a test of warriors, it was a test of the gods.

"I can do it," David said now to the tortured king. "I will fight this Philistine."

"Bah," Saul responded. "He's been fighting longer than you've been alive."

The bears, David said. The lions. God delivered me then, God will deliver me now. I can do this.

The king bent his head in thought. It was a gamble, sending this untested boy into battle. If he was killed, all would be lost. But none other had risen to the Philistine's challenge, and the long standoff had left an expectant tension. Something had to give.

So it was decided. "Take my armor," the king said. But laden with the coat of mail and the heavy bronze helmet, David could hardly walk. He took it off. He would have to fight on his own terms.

David put five stones in his bag, stones worn smooth by the brook. His sling hung from his belt; he held his shepherd's crook like a man out for an afternoon hike.

He crossed into the open. The Philistine took a step toward him. The giant's shield bearer, shorter and nervous-looking, watched David's hands.

A faint smile played on the Philistine's lips. "Am I a dog," he roared across the valley, "that you come after me with a stick? Come and fight. It'll be quick. There will be flesh for the wild animals to eat tonight."

David looked at his opponent. He had never seen such a man – in size, in strength, in armor. He felt naked before such power. He breathed a quick prayer, summoned up his biggest voice, and gave back in bravado: "I come in the name of the Lord of hosts. The God of Israel does not save by sword and spear; but it's *your* body that will feed the birds this day."

The Philistine stepped forward, closer, closer. David found himself running toward him, the blood rushing in his ears. It was as if a force greater than himself was willing his limbs to move. He felt himself reach for a stone from his bag, nestle it in the familiar sling, and whirl it – once, twice, three times, and *now!*

The stone flew straight and true. In an instant it was over. The giant thudded to earth, and David reached for the massive sword.

And remembered. Remembered that even a shepherd has to fight with the weapons he has, has to know what's worth fighting for, has to trust that God will give courage when fear grips hardest. *The Lord is my shepherd. I shall not want.* David remembered the song. Whatever was to come next, he knew he would sing it to summon strength, to seek comfort, to find once again the trust of the Lord: that in the very stones of this good earth, God was at work for God's people and God's promises, and that in the shadow of fear, the light of God shone more brightly than ever.

Forgive or Forget

Genesis   37,   39 - 41

I am Joseph.

Although now, after all these years, it can be hard to remember. I am removed twenty-two years, to be exact, from the callow youth who played his cards wrong and felt the wrath of my brothers at the bottom of a sand pit. Twenty-two years in this land where I am eternally a foreigner, where I must take my meals alone because the Egyptians think it anathema to break bread with a Hebrew.

They gave me an Egyptian name. It means, "God speaks and he lives." Surely God speaks – the God of Israel, not the complex list of gods my neighbors worship. But "he lives" – if he be me, then I'm not so sure. Because for twenty-two years I have been living a death, away from all I loved, away from my mother, away from my beloved father.

Perhaps it was the uncertainty that ate most at my heart. In all these years I never knew who lived and who died, who had succeeded and who struggled on the edge of starvation; I drank at no wedding feasts and sat shivah for no lost souls. In this dry land I have had friends, but at arm's length; I have taken a wife, but more as a trophy than a real companion; I have had sons.

My sons. Only in them have I found a taste of the richness of family that has been so long lost.

The first, Manasseh, has been my joy. Even as he grew out of childhood, he never lost his thirst for fun. He makes me smile, which I so rarely do otherwise. His name means "Forget." Asenath, my wife, suggested it. She knows how I struggle to forget. But as much joy as I take in my firstborn, there is no forgetting. I lie awake nights with twenty-two years of memories.

My second son is the serious one. Ephraim: "Double Prosperity." That was the name I agreed to in a weak moment following his birth. He seems to be determined to follow me as steward of this empire, managing men and grain, keeping hardship from our doors. I have known great prosperity; God has provided, but I have worked hard and used every gift to benefit those who bought me as a teenager. And so in many ways this prosperity has been hollow, because it leaves out Jacob, leaves out Rebekah, leaves out Reuben and Judah and Benjamin and the others, not to say their wives and their children whom I have never held.

I wear a gold chain and the pharaoh's signet ring. I ride in the second-best chariot, and when I pass, they all cry praise. But here is the measure of my happiness: I have two sons. I thought it would be my measure for life.

Strange thing about dreams, the thing that has been my entrée into this royal company. The same dream twice, it is said, means that God has ordained it. It will be so. And so when I dreamed once that my brothers would come to the royal court, it seemed a fable as dreams so often are. When I dreamed it again, I knew what to expect: They would come, they would not know me, they would plead for grain to see them through the famine in Canaan. These brothers who would not say the ritual "Shalom" to me.

But I did not know what to expect from myself. I have always been a planner, a list-maker, a man with goals instead of visions. But as I waited for the dust of the camels to make my brothers' visit known, I decided to be as I am not even with my wife: I decided to wait and see. One cannot regulate the heart.

The interpreter announced their presence. I made sure I wore my finery, to keep the upper hand. They were, after all, beggars with money. Beggars with my own bloodline.

When I saw them, my heart almost broke. But in all the years I had stewed over my fate, I had never come to forgiveness. Maybe the problem was abstraction – it's hard to forgive those whose face one cannot see. But here they were before me, and still I could not forgive.

"Spies," I said. "Why should we trade with you?"

They denied it; I repeated the charge; they denied it again. Thinking back, I am ashamed. They squirmed, and I liked it.

I sent them back to fetch young Benjamin, but kept Simeon as my hostage. I could tell he was frightened. Right in front of me he spoke in words he had no reason to believe I could understand: "We're paying the price," he said, "for what we did to Joseph."

What we did to Joseph. So they remembered. Remembered the brother who "is no more," as they had said. Remembered that they had torn apart our family, broken our father's heart. And over what? The vagaries of dreams – a few images of the world bowing before me – and my father's gift of a coat for me to wear. This face that God has given me, a face that Potiphar's wife found so compelling. Scant excuse for their treachery.

But they remembered, and I found myself overcome. I left by the rear door and did what I had not done for many years – I cried sad and bitter tears.

Still I was not ready to forgive. I filled their sacks with grain, even slipped in the money they had offered, and sent them on their way. Simeon stayed in his cell. I did not visit him.

They had squirmed, and I liked it.

• • •

By the time they returned, I had spent many more nights turning like a door on its hinges. I knew they would come back. The famine was severe, and only in Egypt did we have grain to last seven years. Hunger can drive a man where pride would forbid him go.

I thought of my father and his welfare. And I thought of Benjamin, whom I had not seen since he was a babe in arms – my own brother, whom I should have watched grow up. I was determined to maintain this distance that had become my life. If I wasn't good enough for them at seventeen, how could they expect me to heal what had been broken, heal it now in my prosperous middle age? I had succeeded in spite of them – indeed, in spite of enslavement and prison, in spite of being a stranger in a strange land. My reversals only brought more success, in a strange calculus that many saw as the divine working for good in all my anguish. I wasn't sure about that. Why would progress come with such pain?

And I thought of Yahweh, who saw the betrayal of Eve and made of Eden forever an unattainable homeland, a permanent estrangement from the Almighty. Did God forgive? It seemed to me that the evidence was on the side of justice – that even for God, there are offenses that are beyond fixing.

No one could share my turmoil. Asenath, with her unbroken royal bloodline, could never understand, and anyway our commerce had never reached the level of admitting doubt. Manasseh's light heart would not entertain such agony; and I feared that such talk would destroy Ephraim's carefully cultivated sense of the world's just order. There was no one else. I wrestled alone with my conscience and my God.

When my brothers returned, I had no answer.

They brought gifts – balm and honey, pistachios and almonds – luxuries even we in Egypt have sparingly, because they have to come such great distances. They made a show of presenting them, obeisance to the rich and powerful, bribery for the privilege of trading.

And they brought Benjamin.

Words fail me. He was a grown man, but still I could recognize in his face the spark of the boy I knew so long ago. After all these years!

I could not contain myself. "God be gracious to you," I said, and left the room.

I wept.

At dinner, I made sure Benjamin had a double portion. But of course my table was separate. For all they knew, I was a son of Egypt.

How I came to my plan, I do not know. But I knew if I sent them away again, with no brother as surety, they might not return. I had seen them when Simeon was returned to them, how they wrapped him in their arms as if their family were whole again. *Our* family.

They left at the break of dawn, and my silver divining chalice was in Benjamin's sack. My steward had seen to it.

They were back before noon.

"What can we say to my lord?" Judah cried. His voice quavered; he had heard of the wrath of Pharaoh's court. "How can we clear ourselves?" Then he pleaded for Benjamin's life – surely the joy of his father's old age, and a disaster if he didn't return from Egypt. Some things are worse than starving. Judah even offered himself in Benjamin's place, so great was his fear and his loyalty to our father.

And then – how can I say it? It was as if a mighty dam broke inside me, and the weight of grief and bitterness left me. I called the steward. "Send everyone away," I told him. "Do it quickly."

I was alone with my brothers. They awaited my word of judgment.

I threw off my chain and signet. I looked them full in the face. Still they did not understand.

"May Yahweh forgive me," I said.

"I am Joseph."

• • •

Does God forgive? My scriptures are silent on the question, though the history of our faith is written anew every day. I have learned not to second-guess the Almighty.

But maybe the question should be, what is God's call for our days? I spent twenty-two years in bitterness. That emotional morning in my chambers, they were wiped away like sandstone splitting in two. I knew that I was again with my brothers, and was myself a brother to them, and that I would in time see my father in our homeland. And even with my beloved sons, I had not felt such wholeness. Where there is brokenness, then reconciliation, the honey is twice as sweet.

It is God's blessing, and I can know it again: I am Joseph, son of Jacob, brother to my brothers. In every place, even in this place, I am home.

The Garden

Mark   14:32-42

Blood.
It couldn't be, but there it was. On the sand under his tortured head, the drips and spatters were an unmistakable red. The product of a prayer so intense that it breached the limits of his body.

Not that he was surprised. Nothing surprised him in this rush to judgment. And perhaps that was the worst of all. The knowing. The knowledge of what awaited him on a hill whose outline he could see plainly through the neglected olive trees of Gethsemane.

If there were surprises, he reflected, maybe this all would be easier. Maybe then he could yield himself to one horror at a time, instead of this ordeal of all-at-once strung out over days.

He knelt in the garden and continued.

"Abba," he prayed, almost childlike in his devotion. "Abba, is this the only cup you offer me? Is there no other way?"

He was still a long time, waiting, listening. But only the drone of bees broke the silence, and God seemed far away.

The muscles of his back and legs were in knots. He rose and stretched, unkinking them. It was his habit to pray barefoot, so his skin could touch the good earth. Now he put the battered sandals back on and walked a stone's throw back to the others. To James and John. And most of all to Peter, his rock.

When he came within sight, he stopped short. The three were there, all right. That much cheered him for a moment. They had not fled. But in the hour of his prayer, the hour of his deepest need, they had escaped into sleep.

He watched them for a while. They were like boys, he thought. All bluster and fight, but when night came, they slept like babies. Peter lay face-up in the moss, snoring slightly.

He went to them and laid hands on them, gently bringing them to consciousness. "Simon," he said. "Are you sleeping? You are strong; you are all strong. Keep awake, and keep watch. I need more time." When he left them, he did not look back.

Not that he expected gratitude, he thought when again he was safely by himself. He had learned that early on, when with a touch and a blessing he healed ten men with skin diseases, and only one of them turned with a word of thanks. Indeed, the more he tried to carry out his Father's work, the more people expected of him. It had gotten to the point that he and the Twelve had to escape the crowds by boat sometimes; only the prospect of drowning could keep away the greedy and desperate hands, reaching for him, wanting to touch him or hear a word from him.

He came to his favorite spot, discovered during one of the many afternoons he had spent in the garden. An old olive press, remnant of the day when this was a working farm. Now it lay unused, the thick stone discs weathering in the desert air. A low stone wall had been built around it, and at one end there was an opening in the stones. He nestled into it like a cat in a corner.

So much suffering in the world. Only in the scriptures were there words adequate to express the pain. He had known them from childhood, of course, and so in prayer the old Psalms spoke themselves to the heavens.

"Father," he prayed. "All things are possible for you."

He paused. Did he dare? He knew that God could have a change of heart. His people had seen it with the ancestors. Maybe there was another way.

"Take away this cup from me." Whether he said it aloud or inside, he didn't know.

He listened. Bees. Nothing else.

So much suffering. So much sin.

He sat a long time in silence, thinking about the past three years. It was almost as if the thirty before it didn't exist. When he heard the call and was baptized, it was a birth as surely as the miraculous birth his mother told him about. It was as if he were a fish that finally discovered water. He began, then, to move in God and to breathe God and to act out God. He taught and healed, and he berated those who would make of their faith a ledger of rules instead of an open book of love.

And they responded. There were times when he thought his heart would burst. They were wild with possibilities. A new age seemed to be upon them. He knew he was doing things that no one had ever done, doing them with the power of God. With the daughter of Jairus, even death yielded to that power.

But he had seen crucifixions. Everyone had. The Romans made sure of that. It was a spectacle meant to invoke horror and fear. He had lived with that horror a long time – the crack of delicate bones breaking under the iron spikes, the gasps of the condemned as they grew weaker.

Maybe God would find another way to end it.

He went back to the three. They slept less soundly now, as children fearing a scolding. But they slept.

He knew they were tired. The last days had been an ordeal of travel and confrontation. He could see the whispered plotting as his own people conspired with their oppressors against him. Against them all. No doubt the Twelve were afraid. But it was his body on the line.

"Get up," he said. "Is there no life in you? Keep awake, and keep watch."

He turned on his heel and went back into the garden, deep into the overgrown vegetation. Rough leaves scraped at his sides and face. Oddly, the pain was soothing. It brought him back into the present, where the terrors were less.

Were there angels he could call? Could he invoke a kind of senselessness, as with wine, and so escape the worst of it that way?

Of course there were angels; yes, he could deaden his body. But he knew that would not happen. Because if the plan was to play out, he had to stay true to it. True to God; true to himself.

"Abba," he prayed again. "All things are possible for you. But not what I wish, but what you wish."

And he knew. At that moment, it became clear that the whole of his ministry was pointing to a cross on a hill he could see in the middle distance. He saw that it had to be thus. Because human beings had separated themselves from the Father, and when he tried to show them what God expected of them, they could not bear it. They had to kill the messenger. They had to pour their pain into him because otherwise it would be unbearable. Like the sacrifices at the Temple, all day long animals and birds having their throats cut, he would become the dove killed for peace.

That was clear now. And with clarity came a resolve that he hadn't known before. The answer to his prayer. The bitter cup was his to drink, but now he had the strength to do it.

There would be lashes, he thought as he walked deliberately back toward the others. And humiliation – that was a large part of the shame of crucifixion. And who knew what else? He walked as a condemned man, thoughtful and slow, but steadily toward his future.

Peter, James and John. Sleeping, of course. He knelt beside them and touched their sweating faces. Their eyes opened.

"Get up," he said. "Let us go."

To blood.

And beyond.

One-Course Meal

Exodus   16 : 2 - 15

It was a month after we began our walk through the desert that God gave us the bread of the wilderness. It was a week later that the complaints began.

You know the story. I know it too because I saw it happen. A cook sees many things, being invisible to those of high esteem and many concerns. My tent was near the tents of Moses and Aaron, and so all that came to them passed by me. Cooks should write our histories.

But remember the story. We had barely outrun the excitement of our escape from Egypt. The seers were busy with their sextants and star charts, trying to divine our way across the wasteland that stretched before us. A wasteland with a promise on the other side of it, the promise of a homeland for God's people.

In any human enterprise, it doesn't take long for purpose and resolve to have their sharp edges rounded off. At the end of that first month we had settled into a routine that was comfortable only for its familiarity: rise with the sun, strike the tents and water the animals, pack our scattered belongings, round up the children, and march into the rising sun. In the evening, the sun at our backs, we reversed the process, building fires against the chill desert nights and talking ourselves into sleep with tales of the elders. Aaron had assured us that a land flowing with milk and honey awaited us, but always it was just over the next scrubby hill. Part of the burden (and I laugh now, looking back from a distance of forty years) was that we had walked for a month and seemed no closer to the blessed horizon.

And our provisions were running out. Soon we would have no food.

It is a hard thing for the flesh not to complain against God when the stomach is empty, and so I was not surprised when the people came to Moses that first time. They had been talking – this was before dinner, so their stomach was on their mind – and they arrived with a list of grievances, ready to argue. I stirred my pot – a barley soup tonight, and the last of the Egyptian bread – and listened.

Partly I was worried that they would turn against me; as if I could make food appear from nowhere. But I can say it now – I bore some resentment against these two cousins, who claimed to speak for God but who seemed to be leading us into godforsaken territory. I had thought the words, but never dared say what the protesters now spoke.

"You've brought us into this wilderness only to die of hunger," they said. It was a big crowd, pretty much all the men and some of the braver women, though of course they hung behind. "Why would God want to end our lives this way? Better to have stayed in Egypt, where the bread was rich and plentiful. Even a slave has a full belly sometimes. If God had taken us then, well, at least it would be quick."

I saw Moses and Aaron huddle for a moment. The crowd was restive. Hunger makes a man bold of tongue.

"Israelites!" Moses said. "Your complaint is not against us. It is against God, and that is a grievous thing. But the Almighty has heard your words and heeded them. There will be meat in the evening, and in the morning, bread. Go in peace. God will provide."

Later that night the familiar pattern began. As the sun sank in the west, quails covered our camp, as if a blanket of feathers had descended upon us. It was easy enough to catch a handful, wring their necks and clean and roast them. It made for extra work, but the people were so grateful for the meat, they pitched in.

But the real surprise came in the morning. Before the sun was strong, we awoke to a strange whiteness in the world, as if everything – ground and tent, pack and tether – were frosted in a glistening white.

"There is your bread," said Moses, who usually slept late but this day was up to watch the dew lift with the sun. "Gather it and know that God is with you."

We had to scrape it up with knives, stones, whatever we could find. But all ate their fill, and marveled at the breakfast that appeared while we slept, then vanished as if the heat of the day drew it back into the clouds to be seeds for tomorrow's feast.

"*Manhu*," the people said; "what is it?" The strangeness of that morning demanded an explanation.

"We'll call it manna," Moses said, a hint of irony in his voice. "Get used to it."

♦ ♦ ♦

Over the next little while, we got used to it. Most people said it tasted like a wafer flavored with honey – a taste of the Promised Land, there. What was curious was that it depended on one's age. For young people the manna was like bread; our elders said it tasted like oil; the children spoke only of its honey flavor. Mornings were devoted to gathering the manna; we ground it in mills or pounded it into meal in mortars, then baked it into little loaves.

Bread from the sky. There was enough each day for everyone to be filled; and on the day before the Sabbath, enough for two days, because of course we couldn't gather on the Sabbath.

It was as if the very air fed us, man, woman or child. It was a miracle every morning.

But soon enough, it wasn't.

♦ ♦ ♦

This time they came grumbling to me.

"Every night," they said, "our dreams are full of manna. And then when we rise the stuff is all around. Manna this morning. Manna tomorrow morning. Surely God has something better for us. Why have you not found it?"

"But manna sustains us!" I said. "It's light enough to digest for the day's journey, and surely your health is better – the ailments of Egypt are leaving you."

"We want something different," they said. "We want better."

I saw Aaron and Moses far afield, looking at the crowd but making no effort to approach them.

"Israelites," I said, "where is God's will in this? When you were hungry, you complained. Now God has provided, and again you complain. Do you expect to be feasting like the pharaohs, here in the wildness of the journey?"

"Manna this morning. Manna tomorrow morning," they said again. "Always we are scraping and pounding, and choking the stuff down."

They were right, of course. This I know, as a cook: Variety is its own nourishment. And yet I had no way of giving it to them.

"Very well," I said. "There is meat for dinner, and I hear no complaints about that. In the morning there will be something new for breakfast."

They left me to my fires.

The next morning they were lined up at my tent at the sun's first rays. Heaven knows what they expected. All around us was white like frost, the day's manna like a banquet scattered into the world by an unseen hand.

I handed out the wooden bowls. "Go and wait for God's gift," I said. "God has heard your distress and will not leave you orphaned."

They left with empty bowls and faces like a question mark. I stoked the fire and waited.

Variety is its own nourishment, but hunger can be a savory spice. This I know, as a cook. And so I was not surprised when, one by one, then in little groups, they returned to me, their bowls heaped with grainy white manna ready for pounding and baking. They had tired quickly of this amazing gift, the bread of the wilderness. But when they complained, God indeed gave them variety – the ever-present option of going without.

The day's journey lay ahead, with all its privation and promise. We pounded the manna and shaped it and baked it and ate it. Some said it tasted like wafer. The elders thought they detected a hint of oil. But the little ones, God's promise to every people, they ate their manna with the promise of the Promised Land, and on their lips as they walked was the taste of sweet and hopeful honey.

The Gift in Return

1   S a m u e l   1

ELKANAH

Two women I loved, and two I married.
My father warned against it – "No man
is match for two" – but I was young
and certain of my love and lineage.
The last, at least, bore true.
I am called father now by sons
and daughters; I will go on past death.
Penninah, with her willing wide hips,
has seen to that. And I am grateful.
At time of sacrifice, she gets her share
because she has earned it well.
But Hannah, my sweet and faithful first –
hers is a double portion, for her back
has borne the weight of failure.
Her very name means *grace*, but she
has had so little blessedness.
I know she cries; I love her for that,
for her disappointment of my hopes.
Two women I loved, and two I married.
The one has birthed my joys.
But Hannah I love in sadness.

PENNINAH

It was the Lord who closed her womb
and yet somehow she blamed me.
Was there ever a union of three
where two were not true rivals?
He chose her first, my Elkanah,
and though I filled his ears
with the cries of children,
still she claims a double share
of his affection. Twist the knife.

Our tents stand apart, we eat
at separate tables. With this man,
we anchor a wide triangle.
But we go each year to Shiloh,
to the feast where no one is sad,
and I make sure the young ones
have her know that they are here.
She has her double share
of my husband's fickle heart.
But the Lord has closed her womb.
I won't let her forget.

HANNAH

I weep. But do not think me weak.
The road to Shiloh is meant to be
a road of celebration. We go
to eat and drink, and yes, to praise.
But how can celebration rise
from a heart bitter and bereft?
And how can my sister-wife
glory in such cruelty as draws
my tears from a well of grief?
"Rejoice before the Lord your God
in all you do" – thus says the scroll.
So I smile for my husband
but he sees through me in love:
"Hannah, why do you weep?
Why do you not eat? Why
is your heart sad?" And then: "Am I
not more to you than ten sons?"
Twist the knife. As if heartfire
made up for my empty womb.
As if his words did not echo
with the taunts of a fertile wife.
I forced myself to dine with them
though the festal meal
was bleak on my tongue
and rock in my gut.
And so to temple, and to tears:
"God of the angel armies,
look at my pain and weep with me.
No longer can I live in scorn.
My prayer is only this:
a son to nurse and nurture,

completion for my home.
I offer in my desolation
your gift a gift in return,
my son set apart for the Lord
until his days are ended.
God of grace and justice,
I raise this prayer of hope."

ELI

Drunk, I thought, when I saw her there.
Why this silence before God,
this dumb-show at the holy gate,
if not for wine and plenty of it?
This I have seen before,
dregs of the festival crowd
shaming themselves for show,
sodden in a stronghold of purity.
Her lips moved, and I watched
a long time. Still, no sound,
and I startled her with a touch.
Charge, denial, defense, tears.
"My pain has brought me to the Lord,"
she said. "But even here, no solace."
Something quickened in that space
between us. I am a priest of God
and know the vacant distress
of silence from above. "Child,"
I said, and helped her to her feet,
"may Israel's God grant you favor.
Go now in peace, and live in hope."

ELKANAH

Some perfect circle came around
when Samuel kicked into our world.
The name was his mother's choice,
a private joke with God, she said.
She told me of a promise made,
and love and pride took turns:
the boy would be God's servant,
our sacrifice the glory of the Lord.
Though seeing them as one,
Hannah with Samuel at her breast,
I knew parting would test her faith.
I have, of course, more children;

hers is but one, and she is bound.
One pleads for favor, and sometimes
favor is granted but doesn't stay.
I knew the loss would hurt her.
I dreaded the festival day.

HANNAH
My husband and his household
(yes, *her* as well) were packed for Shiloh,
but I begged to stay behind.
The boy, I said, and held him to my breast,
cannot be left without me yet.
I saw a cloud behind his eyes
but he murmured his assent. They left
and left me with my tender boy.
I held him (almost too big now!)
and nursed my miracle story:
the temple, the prayer, the priest,
this boy whom God had claimed.
What does the God of power need
with one so small? But what does God
require of me? My best, my son. My all.
We traveled light, except for gifts:
flour, wine, and a fine strong bull
born in the year of Samuel.
The sacrifice was made, and then
I led my boy with shaking hand
to temple and the stolid priest
whose blessing came upon me,
those years ago, like rain –
spring rain that sprouts the seeds,
that nourishes the crops
that nourish us, then closes
the covenant with a time of loss,
a gift returned to the giver,
who blesses beyond measure,
who will not be denied.

The Grace Cup

J o h n   2 : 1 - 1 1

I t began as a whisper.

The party had been going for days, a wedding feast that by custom should last for a full week. It was hard to tell where the family ended and the rest of the village began. People came and went, slept at odd hours, tended the children and then went back to the cup and the dancing. Two or three small dogs scurried about underfoot, scrabbling after crusts of bread that fell from the messy tables. The music of lute and drum was in the air.

A fitting tribute to this new couple and this union of families. Here in Galilee, luxuries were rare. A feast like this came only with the joy of the wedding.

But then the householder heard the whispers among the servants, and he saw his steward look at them in disbelief. Could it be that the wine was running out already?

"Without wine there is no joy," the rabbis had said, and the householder knew it. But he knew also that he had a responsibility. Life was hard; they had so few occasions for celebration. It would be a major embarrassment if the party ended too soon. It would dishonor his family. And as these young people began their married life together, such a disgrace would be a curse – a sign of troubles that lay ahead, a grape-colored blotch on their union.

The servants kept up their whispering. The wine was almost out.

The wine, thought Mary. It cannot be.

Another disgrace for the extended family that had brought her a half-day's journey to Cana with her son. She knew that the inner circle of friends sent gifts of wine ahead of time to be poured at the wedding celebration. If there wasn't enough wine, there were too few friends.

If only Joseph had been here to make things right. But her husband was long dead.

A glimpse of the bridegroom and his new wife, unaware of the crisis, still wrapped in each other's adoration. Mary watched them with a twinge of envy. Her own wedding ceremony, three decades earlier, had been brief, and there was no celebration. There were the circumstances, after all. It wouldn't do to feast over a union begun in shame, even if the shame was the town's belief and not their own. She and her husband had only their own certainty about the hand of Yahweh in their lives. It was enough; it was more than enough. But seeing this new bride at the center of celebration, she felt a wistfulness that had become her lot as a wife and a mother. It isn't easy to live a life apart.

The wine, she thought. And turned to her son.

She had seen him handle problems before, and he had done well at supporting her in these years since Joseph's passing. He was there as well with his friends, the five who called themselves his disciples; one of them, Nathaniel, was a child of Cana himself. Maybe Jesus could take up a collection among them. Or maybe, she thought, maybe it's finally time for the prophecy to be fulfilled. Time for the Son of God, whose birth came with stars and angels, time for him to play god in a crisis. His birth was a miracle; could it be time at last for another?

He was at table with his friends. Mary laid a hand on his shoulder.

"They have no wine."

Jesus looked at her carefully, then got up and walked her away from the chattering and the dancing. He bent to address her.

"Woman," he said. "What concern is that to you and me? My hour has not yet come."

Mary fought back a rebuke. The words felt harsh, but in Jesus' eyes there was no sting. They stood together, intimate and silent apart from the crowd. The servants were checking the pantries and shaking their heads. The steward was pointing; his voice, indistinct, rose with an edge of anger.

Mother and son stood as if in discussion, though no words came. Then at last she felt him soften, sensed the turn of acquiescence relax his body. She knew, then. Knew it was time, *his* time, and felt the thrill of inevitability and the fearful awe of what might be next. Because she knew that once it began, it could not be stopped. The hour had come.

She stepped away from him and walked toward the servants. Having exhausted their search for wine, they huddled now in the corner. There would be hell to pay when the supply ran out, any time now.

Jesus saw her speaking to them, saw her point in his direction. He walked over to the group.

"Do whatever he tells you," Mary said, and embraced him, and went back to the table to sit with the women.

Jesus motioned to the servants and led them outside, to a kind of shed attached to the house. It wouldn't do to embarrass the householder with a public show. He opened the door. Inside were six massive water jars, made of stone as the scriptures prescribed, because stone could not be tainted by the filth of the world as clay could.

The jars were half-full, for the guests had done much ritual washing. "He who uses much water in washing will gain much wealth in this world," the saying went, and here at least the host had provided well.

But half-full was not enough. Jesus knew that he could make no half-measures.

"Fill them with water," he said to the servants.

They scurried to the well and brought back jar after jar of clean cool water, pouring them in and then returning for more. Finally the six stone containers were brimfull – 150 gallons of water.

The disciples, missing Jesus, had come around the corner. The water quivered in the jars. The servants stood back in expectation.

What they saw seemed simple enough. This guest of the family laid a hand on the rim of each jar in turn, a touch that seemed to carry both the weight of the world and the lightness of the joyous feast. He touched each vessel, then turned back to the servants.

"Draw some out," he said, "and take it to your steward."

Inside, the steward was working up the courage to approach the bridegroom and say that the wine was gone. He dreaded that moment. The couple looked so happy in the company of all whom they loved, and surely the end of the wine meant the end of the *gamos*, the wedding feast. To have gone to such expense and have it end badly!

But before he could break the news, he felt a tug at his elbow, and one of the servants was there with a flagon of liquid. He drank – a rich and flavorful wine, a vintage that surely should have been served first, when the senses had not yet been dulled by food and drink.

"Where did you find this?" he scolded the servant. "Why did I not know it was there?"

The man led him outside, where the disciples had cups in their hands and fear on their faces. To the steward it was a scene of promise and peril. There was wine enough for ten wedding feasts now. The joy of this couple and their town was complete.

But these stone jars – they were the jars of sacrament. The water they held was reserved for the rites of purification. It had been blessed to that use, blessed to the Holy One. And now this prince of the party, here with his friends, was somehow responsible for wine where there was none, wine where there was only water, the wine of joy intruding on the dutiful obedience that the priests prescribed.

As the steward turned to go back inside, to find the bridegroom and bring him the good news – the best wine saved for last, and more than they could ever need for the most blessed of wedding feasts – he saw the disciples filling their cups, in wonder and in awe, and raising them solemnly toward their friend, and drinking deep of a vintage like none they had ever known.

PART 3

An American Story

Home Talk

An Oneida Community Story

BOSTON, 1904

The old man had been something of a pack rat, and it was late afternoon by the time they got to the back of his closet, where secrets go to be hidden or forgotten.

Why did he keep all this stuff? Elizabeth mused, thinking again of her grandfather as she inhaled the faint tang of pipe smoke from a pile of pilled sweaters. She could hear her grandmother still out in the garage, sorting through the gardening equipment, trying to reduce a couple's life to that of a single, sensible widow. Elizabeth pulled bags and boxes from the closet, dividing the clearly useless from what could be passed on and what her grandmother might want for its sentimental value. She's never been sentimental, she thought. But still …

Beneath a dusty sack of old shoes, her hand bumped against a rough wooden picture frame. Held to the afternoon's fading light, it revealed a handsome young man, in the flush of youth and yet with the unsmiling concentration of photos from the last century. The *past* century, thought Elizabeth, who above all considered herself a creation of this new century, the modern one, where people weren't so hidebound by tradition and religion.

She took the photo to the garage. Her grandmother, Sarah, looked up, panting a little from her exertions.

"Grandmother," said Elizabeth, "who's this?"

Sarah took the photograph in one hand; the other went to her mouth.

"Where did you find this?"

"In the closet. That's not Grandfather."

"I'd forgotten I had this," Sarah said. "It's from a long time ago. A lifetime ago."

"But who?"

Sarah paused and took a long, slow breath. She seemed far away. And then:

"What time is it, dear?"

"Nearly 5."

"This is rather a long story. Shall we go inside? It's time enough for a glass of wine."

ONEIDA, 1866

Thinking back to what had brought him there, Richard Perry remembered the long year he had spent on the west side of Chicago. He had finished college – literature – without any clear idea of what to do next. The Great War was over, so he had no glory to run to. He had been working odd jobs, fixing porches, shoveling snow, to keep body and soul together until he figured it out. It was at the public library, where he whiled away great stretches of time on the pretense of a self-administered graduate school, that he ran across the *Circular*. He began reading, and found he couldn't stop.

In the newspaper's narrow columns he found what he hadn't known he had been searching for: an idea of an ordered life built on Christ, to be sure, but built also on the notion that a man could improve himself continuously and not always be apologizing for being a human being. While the preacher at his somber Presbyterian church was reminding them weekly that "all have sinned and fallen short of the glory of God," this fellow Noyes – for that was the editor of the *Circular* – had an idea that true Christian perfection was within a man's grasp. Not in Chicago, of course. Too many temptations, too much opportunity for backsliding. Along with John Humphrey Noyes, Richard imagined that one day the whole world could become the earthly paradise that the Scriptures foretold. Until then, there was only one place he knew of where it was truly happening: a place in northern New York called the Oneida Community.

As he had seen others do in the thrice-weekly *Circular*, Richard posted a letter of inquiry. Back came the reply from the Great Man himself, along with some pamphlets. Noyes urged him to study the materials, think about it, pray about it, them write back in six months. Six months! For man of twenty-one, it might as well have been six years.

But study he did, and pray, and wait; six months to the day, he wrote a seven-page letter detailing his understanding of Bible Communism. Noyes wrote back promptly with a detained critique. "I sense in your approach something approaching desperation," came the words. "I find great earnestness in your letter, but also a fearfulness that the world is too corrupt. I do not need refugees at Oneida. I need workers – the Lord's workers. If this does not dissuade you, I suggest you spend some more time in prayer and contemplation of the ideals I have set forth." Write again in three months, was the counsel.

He waited. He wrote again. And in three months, Richard Perry, just a few days into his twenty-second year, packed his meager belongings, stowed in its case the viola with which he amused his friends, and set out for Union Station. He changed in Syracuse for the Midland Railroad, and when the locomotive clanged to a stop, he considered it a good sign that the placard read ONEIDA COMMUNITY. He stepped briskly off the platform, put down his things, and looked around for a cart to take him toward utopia.

• • •

For Sarah Thayer, coming to Oneida was less an affirmation than a concession. She was only twenty when her one and only true love had come to a bad end – a love she was sure would be her last as well as her first. He was a pale and serious young man, a boy really, and he had gone off to seek his fortune and never returned. Sarah lived with her father, her mother having passed early from the diphtheria. She knew that wasn't the end of things, but she also knew that in small-town Manlius the choices of a husband were slim. Nor was she entirely certain that wifehood was her calling, at least immediately. It was an era of experimentation; bold ideas were being proposed. She tried hard to imagine what would come next.

It was in that frame of mind that she heard Father Noyes preach for the first time, in a Methodist church in town. She knew something of the odd, insular community a few miles up the road, but like most everyone in town, she knew nothing but dark rumors of its workings and its philosophies. Listening to the Great Man talk, she moved swiftly from skepticism to a general understanding to, by sermon's end, enthusiasm. He spoke of Scripture and his idea that Christ's Second Coming had already happened, back at the time of the destruction of Jerusalem. St. Paul, he said, was a perfect man, and so could we all work toward being perfect. The early church started out in that spirit, but degenerated into hierarchy and dissension. Our Lord's earthly reign, Father Noyes said, can be right here, right now.

He didn't speak of it in church, but she had heard talk of another aspect of the perfectible life: There were no marriages at Oneida. Or rather, there was one "complex" marriage among the two hundred or so adults there. She had guarded her virtue with all the vigor required of a proper young woman, but those early fumblings had left her curious. She wasn't ready to commit herself to one man, but perhaps, she thought, she could commit herself to many.

Within a month, she was settling into her tiny bedroom in the grand Mansion House.

◆ ◆ ◆

When he first saw her, she was at work. Of course. Work was most of the day, whether in the clay-riddled fields of spinach and peas outside the Community or in the printing shop or the trap factory. Work built the soul, the Great Man often said, rather loosely quoting Scripture. It also kept food on the table.

This day, though, was devoted to the Community's first economy, agriculture.

The last frost had broken; it was spring, and they were planting corn, using an ingenious pole-handled device that someone in the trap shop had invented. One plugged it four inches deep, threw a lever, and precisely three kernels were parceled into the good earth.

Like so many big projects, this one was accompanied by the Community band, a kind of fife-and drum corps that played to keep spirits up. A planting bee, the day was called, and pretty much everyone in the Community was there. One thing that had struck Richard in his short time at Oneida: Unlike the laborers he had known in his former life, no one complained much about working. The organizers took care to spread the work around, so that no one toiled too long at any one thing, and the biggest jobs, like this one, were approached almost as a party or an outing. Many hands made light work.

He also had found that the complex marriage for which Oneida was so famous (or infamous) created an almost continuous air of courting. Actual courting, of course, was not allowed. Approaches were done only through intermediaries now, though that hadn't always been the case. But so charged with possibility was each encounter that everyone was on best behavior; the women kept their short hair brushed and their simple clothes neat; the men avoided tobacco, for its effect on the breath.

She was backing around a hedge at the corner of the far field when he quite nearly bowled her over, he was moving so quickly. He reached out to steady her. She drew her breath in sharply.

"I beg your pardon."

"Please don't think me forward. I was afraid you'd fall."

They looked each other full in the face. They stood twenty paces from the nearest other people.

"Richard Perry, at your service," he said, doffing his cap.

She laughed and made a mock curtsy. "Sarah Thayer, milord."

"And how does your corn grow today?"

'With the sun the way it is, we'll be canning by June."

"Didn't I see you in the audience at the orchestra concert on Thursday?"

"Whether you saw me or not, I cannot say. But I was there."

He waited.

"Perhaps you'd like some criticism on your playing," she ventured.

"All right."

"Technically, it was fine. The Mozart especially – very neatly done. But I do wish you would put more *fire* into your playing. It left me cold. . . . Now, to my work."

She left for more seed. And Richard Perry thought, you, milady, are next.

• • •

It was at orchestra practice the following week that he thought again of her words. Mutual criticism was deeply ingrained in the Community; without it, Father Noyes said, no one would climb the ladder of ascending fellowship toward perfection. But Richard had enough stubbornness left in him to resist. Silently, of course. One could not reply except to recognize that a criticism was well taken.

He had not yet been through a formal criticism, which was generally conducted by four or five members chosen by Noyes and trained in the art of correction. But there had been a few instances of private conversations, criticisms-in-passing. They hurt, he had to admit it. He had prayed about it, and tried to take good advice to heart, but he knew he must be a long way from enlightenment, because his spirit was rebellious.

And now Sarah's words. Fire. If she wanted fire, he could burn with the best of them. As the orchestra launched into a Beethoven piece, he hit the strings hard, turning his wounded heart toward the notes and the bow. His fingers ached for gripping the viola's neck so tightly. But he played beautifully, powerfully. He knew it.

"Diotrephiasis."

"What?"

"That's what Father Noyes calls it," said the cellist to his left, whose name was Earl Miller. "When you try to play better than other people, I mean. You play beautifully, Richard. But remember: Father Noyes plays violin, and he's not very good. You don't want to show him up. Did you ever hear of Frank Wayland-Smith? He was a tremendous violinist. He loved that instrument. So much so the Father Noyes called him in and said his playing was interfering with his other obligations to the Community. He made him hand over his violin, his music books, his sheet music – everything. Noyes put them away in his closet."

Richard thought about this. He spoke carefully: "But is it not the goal to improve in all ways, including one's art?"

"Improve, yes. Excel, maybe not," Earl said. "I just think you might want to be careful. I couldn't imagine life without playing my music. I have to limit my practice time to be sure. Moderation in all things, you know. My impression is that Father Noyes would rather have a mediocre orchestra that doesn't provoke the members to jealousy, than the New York Philharmonic there in the Mansion Hall."

◆ ◆ ◆

Despite the prohibition against courting, Sarah and Richard courted. They did it with a glance across three rows of benches at the Nightly Meeting. He sat across from her in the incessant self-improvement classes that were organized around studying French, or phrenology, or Scripture. He waltzed with her at the Friday evening dances, being careful also to give the older women a whirl on the dance floor as well; alliances among the young, at the expense of their assumedly spiritually superior elders, were frowned upon. She chose him as a partner in the endless games of croquet that formed on the South Lawn.

It was all quite proper, and it was all quite exciting. He knew he shouldn't, but he thought of her, and her alone, late at night before falling into an exhausted sleep. Selfish, such thoughts were called. Contrary to the good of the Community.

He couldn't help it. He loved the Community and its people, he loved Sarah. He could not make them mean the same thing.

◆ ◆ ◆

My dear Harriet Skinner,

I humbly beseech your assistance in arranging a social encounter with Miss Sarah Thayer. I believe that she and I both would benefit from the practice of pleasure-giving such an encounter would afford, and you are aware of my efforts toward improving my skills in this area. Miss Thayer is my spiritual superior, by virtue of her longer tenure here in the Community and her being my senior of eight years, and assuredly this represents an opportunity for improvement on my part which I solemnly desire.

I await your decision, and Sarah's, and I give you my thanks.

Your servant in Christ Jesus,

Richard Perry

◆ ◆ ◆

He waited: three days, four days. An agony. Five days, six. Finally, on a Monday evening after a day in the trap shop, a typical meatless dinner and a chess game at which he lost badly, he went into his bedroom to find a small piece of paper, folded, on the nightstand. He opened it. It was Harriet Skinner's personal stationery, and on it was a single word. Yes.

◆ ◆ ◆

They sat together the next night at Evening Meeting. It was Tuesday, so that meant a lecture from Mr. Noyes. On this occasion it was a reading from *The Berean*, Noyes' pamphlet setting out his principles for the Community; they studied it seriously as the Scriptures, and hearing Noyes discuss its intricacies was like hearing St. Paul himself talking about the writing of his epistles. But on this night, Richard could hardly hear the Great Man. Blood was rushing in his ears. He concentrated on Father Noyes' great white beard; he studied the figures painted on the high ceiling to represent Justice, Music, Astronomy and History. He looked at Sarah's hands, trailed across them with his own once or twice only to be brushed aside. He waited.

Finally the Home Talk ended. Sarah announced to the woman on her other side – special friendships weren't allowed, of course, but Richard knew that this woman, whose name was Mary, was Sarah's frequent companion – that she would be skipping the games tonight and going to her bedroom. She left. He waited a few minutes, then climbed the stairs to the second floor.

She had left the door open a crack, and when he knocked it swung in. She was sitting on her narrow bed, her legs bare, still in the knee-length skirt all the women wore. He closed the door behind him. There was no lock.

"Sarah."

Father Noyes' rules for social intercourse specified that one wasn't to talk much. It took away from the spirituality of the moment. She looked up at him.

"I knew you would apply for me. There's something that's rather funny, Richard. I applied for you as well. Harriet received our notes on the same day. All this time she's held them."

"'Anticipation sweetens the appetite.' Didn't I read that somewhere?"

"You read too much."

Trembling, he went to her, knelt like a supplicant, and began.

• • •

The next month was the happiest he had known, in a Community where happiness was expected and the deep sadness of "hypo" was considered the Devil's work. They saw each other daily, even to the point where Richard, who generally considered children more pests than people, volunteered to help in the Children's House because Sarah had been assigned there for a few days. They met in her room twice a week, on Wednesdays and, scandalously, Sundays; they joked about being "like an old married couple." But of course they had little knowledge of what married couples did; they knew only the one marriage in which they all lived in Oneida, and which had come to seem the only possible arrangement.

Among the tourists from outside the Community who made sightseeing at Oneida their weekend outing, they saw couples their own age, hand in hand, laughing at each other's jokes and knowing that they would return home that night to their own bedroom and sleep the night through beside each other. For Sarah, so deeply enmeshed in the communal spirit, this seemed almost an affront. She looked at these women visitors, yoked in obedience to one man for better or worse, and thought: One choice, and then no more choices. One pleasure, or set of pleasures, for a lifetime. What kind of love would bring one to enlist in such a life? How could these women see the perfectible pleasures of Oneida – yes, including the social ones – and not despair over their choices?

Then she would see Richard looking at the same couples, and an uneasy feeling would come over her, because she was coming to know that there was trouble here. He looked at the young marrieds, and she knew he was thinking: A whole lifetime of nights to worship one perfect woman. Where else could one find such a lifetime's happiness?

♦ ♦ ♦

He tried to control his feelings, both loving and dark. Had he become a better man through Sarah? He thought yes. But he knew his commitment had gone too far. He knew it because he felt bile rise in him when she walked in the gardens with another, or smiled when one of the older members looked her way. She had other social engagements, of course. Everyone did. And everyone knew who was with whom. By design of the buildings and by practice of philosophy, there was no privacy in the Community. He was tormented, when not with Sarah, by thoughts of her in another's arms. He tried not to be nearby when her door closed behind her.

♦ ♦ ♦

One Sunday, the social engagement went wrong.

He had, of course, practiced male continence, Father Noyes' technique for separating the amative and the procreative purposes of the act. Like all male members in their early stages, he had been introduced to complex marriage through the older women in the Community. He had erred a few times in the early going, but soon mastered the rhythms and dangers of the technique. Like rowing near the edge of a waterfall, as Noyes was wont to describe it. Richard hadn't gone over the brink in months and months.

Perhaps it was possessiveness; perhaps it was the curve of her shoulders seen in a light he had never noticed before; perhaps it was something inside him giving way to the Devil. This time, passion won out. He had failed the Community; he had failed her.

Sarah was furious. "How could you?" she hissed. She was curled into a ball in the room's one chair, a rocker. "You knew, and you didn't stop."

"I couldn't." Richard knelt at her feet, near tears. "I am sorry. I meant no disrespect. It's just ...This happens between men and women."

"Not here," she snapped back. "Here it's by design, not by brute force and happenstance."

"I was wrong," he said miserably. "I'm weak, I'm not perfect."

"Nor am I," she said, seeming to soften. "Nor is any of us. But to give in – not to try – Richard, that is sin. You've made me the Devil's handmaiden."

"I *can't* be perfect," he said. "Maybe you can get there. I cannot. What's more, I don't suppose I *want* to be perfect. Isn't it an affront to God, to imagine ourselves sinless?"

"Not according to Father Noyes. He says it's our duty. If we live with Christ in our soul, we won't be tempted.

"Christ was perfect. Look what it got him."

"Richard!"

He stood. "I'm sorry. That was wrong. God help me, I'm not trying to be base and evil and contrary. It's not that I'm trying to sin. It's just against human nature to be perfect."

"But it's God's nature. You're not trusting God enough."

He stood. "I'll do better next time."

"We'll see."

• • •

Two days hence, at Evening Meeting, they were called up for mutual criticism.

Before the assembled members, they sat in hard wooden chairs facing Mr. Noyes' committee of four men. Henry Seymour began, as was the custom, directly.

"Sarah, Richard, you are both honorable people and fine members of the Community. Sarah, we are especially glad of your work with the children; you show great empathy for them. And Richard, I know you've been working hard to conquer your musical ambitions, and the others in the orchestra tell me that you've become less likely to disrupt its harmony by intruding your own playing to the fore."

Abram Smith: "We are concerned about the claiming spirit in your social relations. We have seen much closeness between you. Of course, this is a good thing. But we think that it may be interfering with your other obligations to the Community, especially to the other members whom you do not choose to favor with your pleasures."

Otis Miller: "Selfish love is not love, brethren. It is misdirection of God's gifts for one's own sake and not for another's pleasure. It is wrong."

"Do you have any response?" Seymour asked.

Sarah shook her head, her eyes downcast. She knew they were right. Perhaps the most fearful aspect of the criticism is that they were always right. It was as if they had special insight into the soul.

"And you, Richard?"

He gathered his thoughts and looked hard at Seymour. "It may be true that I have seen too much of Sarah," he said carefully. "But I have done my share of the work in the Community, and that includes the amative work. For that it is, brethren, when one's appetite is not there: work.

"And why must we persist in the idea that a particular love is dangerous when a general love is ideal? I fail to understand why God's greatest gift is called selfishness."

"God's greatest gift," roared the last inquisitor, John Hutchins, "is his people living in community. Forget not Jesus' words, 'Where two or more of you are gathered in his name, there am I also.'"

"Two or more," Richard said. "Or just two."

"More faithful, more of God's love. He did not give you talents to squander them on one person among a billion." Sarah winced. *Squander.*

"In the Community, we are not to have close friendships even of our own sex. Does this promote intimacy – God's intimacy? Does not the Lord wish us to love each other fully? And how can we do so without the freedom to form attachments? Is yours a God at arm's length?"

Smith took for himself the last word. "Brother, we sympathize with your feelings. But you should know by now that what matters is all of us, not some of us. God gave us this land, these orchards, these buildings, to use for his glory. They are not playthings. Nor are his people to be playthings. We must cherish each one, and practice pleasure for all. The criticism is finished. Richard, study *The Berean* this week."

• • •

Two weeks into a halfway knowledge, she had to be sure. She borrowed a traveling suit of clothes from the tailor shop – kept there for journeys out of the Community, though these were rare – and rode by train all the way to Syracuse. There she walked into the first doctor's office she saw and asked for an appointment. She rode back to Oneida pale, and frightened, and somehow filled with joy.

• • •

They sat in one of the smaller common rooms, dubbed the Plant Room because one of the members who fancied himself a horticulturist had furnished it with greenery ordered from Connecticut. Or rather, Sarah sat. Richard paced.

"This isn't supposed to happen at Oneida," he said. "Father Noyes won't like it. He won't like a real child among the stirps."

"It happens," she said. "And what do you mean, a real child? Every child is real."

"I mean a child whose birth is chosen by God and not by John Humphrey Noyes," he said grimly. "It's not natural that he should do the choosing."

"Father Noyes has studied it," Sarah replied. "He knows what traits to combine, what personalities can produce a better kind of person ..."

"A child who will grow up to be perfect? Like Mr. Noyes?"

"That's the idea, I suppose."

"So what was it that produced Mr. John Humphrey Noyes, the perfect man?" Richard said bitterly. "Stirpiculture? Our just our dumb luck?"

"God's hand," she replied. "But that's no reason man cannot intercede on God's behalf. God didn't create Bible Communism, did he? He created the Bible, and it took a man to interpret it and understand that Perfectionism was his will for us."

Richard paced some more. Through the small window, they heard the merriment of the croquet players.

"I cannot go on at arm's length," he said finally. "I love you. I need to be by your side, without apology. I need to be this child's father."

"Richard," she said, and thought how to say what she knew she must. "I feel it, too. Being with you has been like looking over the far hill into the great world. But that world is not my world. I am not so strong as you. I cannot make the choices you make and not feel regret. If I were to marry you and leave Oneida, I would always regret what I would leave behind here. The people. The lovers. Father Noyes. The sense that this experiment, this Community, could be the thing that will make Christ's rule on earth real and true and present. I must stay here. It's God's call for me. I've felt it from the first, and nothing – not even you, not even this child – changes that."

"And me?"

"Remember when Jesus met the rich young man? 'Sell all you have and give the money to the poor,' he said. He couldn't, but you can. You have to be able to give up the thing you hold dearest. It's what our Lord asks of you, Richard. You daren't disobey."

{ 113 }

ONEIDA COMMUNITY. A solitary figure stood waiting as the westbound train pulled into the station. So much hope, he thought, concentrated into so few souls. Could their plan for a little piece of New York indeed be God's plan for the world? They would all know soon enough, he figured. In the meantime, he would spend some time thinking, maybe studying, maybe traveling. There was a lot to see beyond that far hill. The locomotive screeched and huffed to a halt. The doors opened. Richard stepped up into the first car, out into an imperfect world.

BOSTON, 1904

The heat of the afternoon had given way to the gentle glow of an early September evening. A bottle stood empty; another was on its way there.

"Richard," Elizabeth said. "That's him in the picture?"

"Yea, dear," said Sarah. "Father Noyes had a photographer come 'round once a year, and I had someone in the darkroom make me one. For a while, I couldn't bear not looking at it; then I couldn't bear looking. I put it away."

"Grandmother ... the child?"

"Your mother." She sipped. "Your grandfather, God rest his soul, adopted her when she was a year old. She never knew any different, and still doesn't to this day." She looked sharply, meaningfully, at Elizabeth.

"But Oneida –what happened?"

"I left when the baby was still at my breast. It was the practice to take children, once they were weaned, and put them in the Children's House. Their mothers and fathers would see them specially for only a couple of hours a week. I couldn't bear the thought of that."

"I don't understand."

"You wouldn't – or won't, until you become a mother. Then you'll know. That child was a part of me. She had been inside me, and in a sense she still was. Before she was born, I was sure that Father Noyes had the right idea, about children as well as about most other things. Share the work of bringing them up, and they'll grow into stronger parts of the Community. But I just couldn't. I couldn't let go of her."

Tears glistened in two sets of eyes.

"Did you ever see Richard again?"

"Never. When I resigned from the Community, I left no forwarding address. And within a year I had taken your grandfather's name. There was no way for Richard to know I would be in Boston, no way for him to find me."

She paused.

"It was a different time. We were sure we were God's best hope on earth. And it didn't go wrong, exactly, but it just didn't turn out to be exactly right."

She took the picture. "I have no regrets, Lizzie. Live so you can say the same. Now I want to see if you can keep a secret. Let's walk over and visit your mother."